IN MY
SANDBOX

RUDY FEDERMAN

Cover art by Michael Federman
Copyright © 2010 Rudy Federman
All rights reserved.

ISBN: 1451568029
ISBN-13: 9781451568028

PREFACE

When I was twelve, I dreamed of a place called Vandenberg. Rockets were launched from there. It was a place of wonder and the revealing of the unknown. The era of rockets, satellites, and space exploration had begun and I wanted to be a part of it—somehow.

This book is meant to be an inspiration. It's a string of stories about innocence, wonder, challenge, disappointment, and success. Most importantly, it is a story of a boy growing to manhood and his life experiences. A boy that didn't excel in his early school days but eventually found his scholastic niche. A boy who was many times told to accept what he had been given and deal with it—ergo, don't try. A boy who succeeded in spite of the uphill challenges. That boy was me!

This book focuses on the important people and events that shaped me through the years. It touches on the spiritual. It tries to show that even though the environment of my origin would ordinarily imply a route of failure or mediocrity, I was fortunate to shake off the stigma and move on. I made it.

For all those who have helped shape my life, thank you. I wasn't left on the vine. Because of you I strove to take each day and make it a victory. The title, *In My Sandbox*, has multiple meanings. It accurately notes the real place of my play as a young boy, where I experienced a memorable and unexplainable spiritual event that has stayed with me through life. It also represents a simple beginning that everyone can identify with.

This book is based on my actual life occurrences. The dialogue appearing in this book is taken from memory; however, in some cases it was enhanced for the reader. In a few instances the names of the characters have been changed to protect their privacy.

This is a book about hope, victory, and most importantly—love.

To my wife, Anita
my sons, Michael and Jason, and their families
and, of course, Mom and Dad
I love you all

PROLOGUE

A little boy alone
Sits just outside his home
Wondering

It was a late spring day in 1949. He sat alone, as always, this time in his sandbox near the southwest corner of the little white cracker-box house called home. His mom put him there often on warm days as she went about her business. It was safe and she knew the boy would be okay. It really wasn't the best sandbox—simple old wooden slats nailed crudely together at the corners. The sand was from the small garden only a few feet away. Mom did her best to provide a play area. It did the job. Toys were rare, too—just one. A block of wood with wires for axles and thread spools for wheels. That and a great imagination were all that was needed. It was enough—it had to be.

The mid-morning sun was filtering through the long pine needles from the thicket of giant white pines in the backyard. It was warm and comforting. A slight but warm spring breeze made a swishing sound through the trees, but it wasn't loud enough to cover the sounds of the eager birds going about their spring tasks. An occasional blue jay would squawk and provide the only interruption to what would typically be a serene picture of calm.

Today, however, there was no calm. Harsh sounds of anger from inside. Sounds of slamming doors, furniture being shoved, and loud voices penetrated the thin uninsulated walls of the house. This had happened before, but this time seemed different. It was louder and meaner. The walls of the house failed to keep the harsh sounds inside. The little boy started to cry, wishing they would stop. He was very young, but already memories of strife, turmoil, and tension were being etched into his brain. A feeling of loneliness and fear overcame what should have been sensations of love and security.

He sat there, alone, holding back tears and trying to ignore the noises from within the house. He knew he was supposed to stay where he was placed by his mom. He had no desire to disobey. He had just that one toy to play with, but it wasn't enough to keep him from the sadness he felt inside.

Out of the corner of his eye he saw two women approaching him, seemingly from out of nowhere. He certainly hadn't noticed them before now. The sun was shining on their backs as they approached, creating a kind of halo-like aura around them. They apparently came from the country lane which ran directly in front of the house. Perhaps they had heard the noises from inside and were coming over to see if he was okay. He wasn't sure. Strangers would typically frighten him, but for some reason not this time.

He looked up at them as they approached. The gleaming sun shimmering through the trees above them prevented a clear view of their faces. He could tell they were smiling and looked very friendly, but he indeed had never seen them before. They came to the sandbox and knelt down on its edge. They seemed nice enough. They didn't utter a sound to the boy or each other—just looked at each other and smiled as if they knew the other's thoughts. There was an over-powering yet acceptable strangeness about them.

The lady on the left looked older and was much heavier than the other—a little shorter, too. Her gray hair was in a bun placed on top of her head, much like older women did then. Her skin was pleasantly wrinkled. Her blue dress with white dots matched a knitted shawl draped over her rounded shoulders. She looked like a grandma. The other lady was slim and wore a plain tan dress with no trim. She had long brown hair that fell well below the shoulders. A pleasant-looking woman with caring brown eyes and a small smile on her thin lips. She seemed too young to be a grandma, unlike the other lady. They continued to look at the boy, and then at each other several times.

A moment after they knelt down near the boy, a quiet seemed to suddenly spread around the sandbox. The calm of the day started to return.

The older lady reached out her right hand and caressed the boy's tear-wetted left cheek. Her pervasive warm smile and a loving look communicated calm and caring from the depths of her gray-blue eyes. The other lady continued her knowing smile and looked on. The boy, completely unafraid, stopped crying and began to smile back at them. Something special was happening. He never heard them speak, but as she touched his face he heard a voice in his head.

"There now, it is alright. Don't be afraid, for your future is bright," she said. The peace of the moment continued.

Wondering what was happening inside, he looked toward the house and then back at the ladies, but they were gone. They were nowhere in sight. They left as mysteriously as they arrived. Where did they go? The boy felt different now. In what seemed like an instant the world around him changed. No more noises from the house. The calming sounds of the birds and breeze returned. It was okay, just as the lady had said. But where did they go? Who were those women? Whoever they were, they left an impression on this young boy that would stay with him for the rest of his life.

As the boy grew into manhood he would always remember that day, when two ladies came for a visit and calm was restored. He also never forgot the unspoken words he heard from a voice inside: "It is alright. Don't be afraid. Your future is bright."

What follows is a compilation of stories of this little boy's life that were likely shaped by the event of that special day in the sandbox.

"The Little Boy"

ONE

A simple place
Life was hard but good
Memories

It was a small town in West Central Wisconsin—a sleepy little place with a population between two and three thousand where everyone knew everyone and nearly everything about them. The town was the county seat and provided reasonable shopping conveniences, and a place for the many farmers to barter their crops harvested each year. A river dividing the township flowed from the north to the south, draining into the Mississippi River some forty miles further south. Now, here was a concept: it was called the Black River—yup, because the water looked black. Wasn't that original? The downtown Main Street wasn't long, only five blocks, but rose from the riverbanks on the east to the big hill on the west end of town. You could parallel park on either side, with just enough room in the middle to accommodate two narrow lanes originally meant for horse and wagon. At the high end of the street was a huge Catholic church made of gray-white granite. It towered over the entire town and surrounding area. You could see it from just about everywhere.

We had the usual stores any small town would have back then. Seems all the old stores there had squeaky wooden slat floors—merchants always knew if there was a customer in the store. All the stores then had their own reason for being—their own personality. The drugstore sold drugs, but had a soda fountain for a cherry coke or a root beer float. The hardware store just sold nails, tools, etc., and the merchant was always on hand and knew everything about what he had in stock, and knew you well enough to recommend just the right tool.

There was an old movie theater where Saturday matinees cost fifteen cents—usually a double-feature oater with a newsreel and a cartoon. Down the street from there was a bar and a two-lane bowling alley. There was a bank on either end of Main Street. I always wondered why we needed two. There must have been money somewhere. Farmers' shopping days were usually on Saturday and the town was pretty busy then. What stood out to me was the dime store or the Ben Franklin five-and-ten. Near the double doors and to the right as you entered was a well-used bench with chipped paint. Womenfolk, with their tote bags, would meet in the dime store and discuss the ways of the world while watching the toddler children ride a funny-looking machine representing a horse that only went up and down. The ride would last a minute or two and that was it. It cost a dime—go figure. I never understood why a kid got such a kick out of sitting on that thing. I tried it once but got no joy! The menfolk could usually be found at the bar across the street, under the guise of waiting for their grain to be processed just two blocks away or for the women to finish their shopping. It usually took a couple of beers to wrap up the weather and all the crappy things going on in Washington, then they were ready to find their women and head back to the farm, looking forward to next week for another round of beers, politics, and weather.

Most of the folks were simple and hardworking. It seems like all the townsfolk and visiting farmers had definite attitudes about life firmly ingrained by their years of hard life, or transferred to them by European immigrant parents who came over to make a good, honest living in this land of opportunity. There ain't no free lunch and you work for what you get. Even today, the people back there share those valuable tenets.

Over the river was a huge quarter-mile-long bridge high above the water at least a hundred feet, where strolling tourists were always seen stopping midway to snap a picture of the river far below and the historic dam just upstream.

In our early teens, we used to cross the river "under" the bridge by holding on to only one rather thick steel support cable which ran the span of the bridge. It was barely possible for us to have a firm grasp while placing our feet one ahead of the other on a narrow structural I-beam plate. We would feel the shaking of the structure as heavy trucks passed overhead. Surely, we had no idea the danger involved. The distance to the water and rocks below was so far that people fishing looked like ants. Should we have fallen it would have been sure and sudden death. It was dumb but we didn't care—we were invincible (and lucky). Had our parents known of these escapades there would have been hell to pay.

The massive, rusty-red granite boulders strewn on the riverbed and below the dam provided evidence of the much-talked-about 1911 great flood, which carved out a vast canyon and wiped out most of the downtown area. In dry years, these boulders served well as platforms to jump on to hopscotch across the water. They also gave way to excellent fishing spots. In the winter, the ice floes would build huge bergs that cascaded over the dam's spillway. Just above the dam was what remains of an early railroad trestle. The wood support beams were long gone, but the concrete foundation rising some thirty or so feet above the water was still there and provided daring youth with a jumping-off platform into the river below. This view was our town's main attraction year-round, but in the winter the ice and snow, along with the seasonal decorations of Christmas throughout town, transformed this little place into a Currier and Ives wonderland.

Christmas was indeed a most magical time of year in our town. People throughout town seemed different at that time; friendlier, I think. The folks that never seemed to have the time of day for you suddenly smiled and said hi. Downtown, the trimmings crossed Main Street at every light pole, the stores were always decorated with bright lights only seen at that time of year, and at noon Christmas songs rang out from the Catholic church up the hill for a week before the big day. The movie theater always offered special holiday matinees every Saturday for a month before Christmas. Everyone in town seemed happy during that time of year, as if they still believed in Santa Claus.

At our house, Mom would find a tree in the nearby woods and nail the base to a makeshift stand. She liked to get the kind with short needles—spruce, I think. Then she would search the only closet in the house to find the old boxes with all those overused decorations. She would hand out the decorations to each of us a little at a time so we could help decorate. Those decorations were obviously very old, but we couldn't afford anything new. The red window wreaths with a light in the middle were faded to an orange, but we didn't care. They worked! Mom would even pop some corn so we could make popcorn strings for the tree. It was always a struggle to make the strings and not eat the popcorn as we made them. Once finished, we would all sort of stare quietly at the tree each of us had helped create and gaze wantonly while tucked away in our own mental hiding place of Christmas expectation. I used to lie on the floor with my head well under the tree and stare up through the limbs and decorations, mesmerized by the flashing greens, reds, and blues and the smell of fresh pine. The strands of lead tinsel would tickle as they drooped down near me. All of these things transformed our little home into a place of joy and hope, and matched the magical glee which typically spread throughout the entire little town at that very special Christmastime.

Aside from Christmas and all the wintertime high points of holiday emotions, ours was a very modest abode that transmitted the message of poverty to all who gazed upon it. We lived on the east side of the river about two miles from the bridge. The entire town and surrounding area were never classified as a place of high society and wealthy people, although every town around had a couple of wealthy families, and in this regard our town was no different. One could summarize that the whole area was a simple place for hardworking folks to live and raise their families. Nevertheless, everything being relative, ours was the "poor side" of the river—the east side. All those with more money (which was just about everyone) apparently lived on the west side. This economic distinction provided a cause for the "richer" west-siders to give those of us on the east side a name for our area. Hartsgravel, they called it! Don't know exactly where that name came from, but we all knew it wasn't meant as a compliment.

Dad had left long ago, when I was two. Mom did what little she could to provide for us, and eked out a living by working as a waitress at a nearby truck stop and taking in laundry for soldiers from a military camp nearby.

The house wasn't much. Just the four of us—Mom, my two older sisters, and I—lived there. It was a little white wood structure comprised of three rooms, with a cranny or recess for a kitchen that was not really a room. The only thing that made the place seem roomy was the lack of much-needed furniture. The building came from somewhere west of town. They must have gotten a good deal on the place—and should have!

The smallest room was the only bedroom. I slept in a crib in the same room as Mom from infancy to around five. My sisters shared a roll-away cot in the middle room. Beyond the little bedroom and the next was the largest room, with a wood-burning stove off to one side as our main heating source. The kitchen recess was to the right of the heater. In there was a small two-burner electric hot plate for cooking, an icebox with big blocks of ice in the top compartment, and a little counter with a sink which drained into a pail (which we called the slop bucket). There was no running water. Our water either came from our neighbor's outside pump or our little green pitcher pump that was about eighteen inches high and attached to the countertop of the sink area. A pail of water with a ladle was always next to the pump for the necessary priming prior to pumping. The well for the pump was straight down below the floor in the hand-dug cellar directly beneath the nook.

The cellar extended under the nook but was mainly below the large room. Now that cellar was a place of many memories, mostly scary ones. In the middle of the nook floor and near the entrance to the larger room from the nook was the cellar access hole, or trapdoor, cut like a porthole into the abyss of the dark, dank, and creepy unknown. No stairs for easy access, just a crude wooden ladder running straight up and down extending from the trapdoor hinge area to the bottom and resting on a square concrete slab to prevent it from sinking into the sandy floor. In the far end was a light bulb hanging from a single cord that was attached to one of the beams of the floor above. It was impossible to reach the light until after descending to the bottom of the ladder and feeling your way across the sandy floor. This was where Mom stored canned food and wood for the stove.

The trapdoor had a recessed pull ring on it to aid in opening. It was too heavy for me to lift, but whenever Mom went down there I would scurry over to look—wondering if I could see not only what she was doing but if there indeed was something or someone down there. It was an eerie place, but somehow I had to know what was down in that dark hole. It was scary; I remember hearing strange scraping noises from the cellar—like things moving around. When the trapdoor was down I would often go and put my ear on top of it to listen—something was definitely down there. Now, I will never admit that I believed in the boogeyman, but I was convinced he lived down there. Whatever might have been down there, somehow I knew it was safe when Mom was home. She never seemed scared to go into the cellar. Maybe it was because whenever she went down there those noises stopped. I wondered why they did. What powers did Mom have?

I used to peer over the edge whenever Mom went in it, to confirm my suspicions or reassure my safety. Besides, it was fun to see everything upside down, too. Mom worried that I would fall and scolded me whenever I got too close—which was virtually every time that access hole was open.

"Keep him away from the hole. I will be right back up. I'll just be a minute," she said to my sister. Sis was supposed to watch me whenever Mom had to go down there, but she couldn't catch me all the time.

Oh, the inevitability of it all. One day when hanging over the edge and looking down, I scooted too close to the edge, losing my grip on it and falling headfirst down to the base of the ladder, my head hitting the cement slab. I hit with a hard thud; it must have sounded like a bag of potatoes. I didn't scream—it was over almost before it began. But there I lay—out cold! I am sure Mom thought I was dead until she saw that I was breathing. I woke up later upstairs, wondering what had happened but feeling strange. To bring down the swelling, Mom had put a cold butter knife on the rather huge bump manifesting itself on my forehead, just above my eyes. I must have looked like some alien creature. By the look on her face I wasn't sure if she was mad for what I did or just worried about me. I think the latter. Looking into the mirror I hardly recognized me. I had no memory of the fall. There was no phone then, no ambulance. So whatever the emergency we were pretty much alone. I was fine that time, but I never again went near the hole in the floor where the boogeyman lived. Oh, those noises were real; they were from the mice and rats that made it their home mostly in the wintertime—not from the boogeyman. It sure would have been a lot easier on me if I had known about them in the first place. The boogeyman got way too much billing—but then, I never believed in him anyway. Yeah, right.

Years later, the back part of the cellar would be where I set up my laboratory to do many "top secret" experiments in chemistry and physics. On one occasion, I was in that part of the house when Mom and Dad were out of town for the weekend, and I wanted to experiment. I created a smoke bomb that scared the crap out of me. It was so thick, I could hardly see. I opened the windows. Neighbors came running with buckets, thinking we were on fire. We weren't—just smoky. I got the damned thing out of the house and thanked God it wasn't worse. Mom and Dad never knew!

Winters were brutal. Temperatures in the dead of winter would often go well below zero. Two times in my youth it was recorded as minus fifty-two degrees.

Did you ever toss a pail of boiling water outside in the air when it was that cold? I did. It was an explosion of ice and steam. Water freezing before it hit the ground. Look, one has to entertain oneself where it is possible. What else can you do when it is that cold outside?

The wood stove in the largest room was replaced eventually with an oil-burning stove. This was a big improvement, since it had a circulation in the rear to blow out the hot air. The uninsulated house would fall below freezing in the outer areas away from the heater. Mom would have to get up earlier than the rest of us to stoke the fire chamber and increase the flow of oil, which came from a tank with a supply tube penetrating the wall. Sometimes, when the temperature outside was especially cold, the oil in the line would get thick and flow so slowly that the fire would hardly exist.

Do you have any idea what happens to fuel oil when it is fifty-two below outside? Jelly—that's what! The supply line clogs with thickened oil and the only way to get it to flow is to heat up the line. That, too, is a challenge.

After a bit, and with the heat as high as it would go and the side panels wide open, we would race to dress. I usually won. Girls have more things to put on! We weren't naked long. No, we weren't bashful—just cold.

In front and to the east of the house was an unpaved country road. Directly across the road was an open field forested all around its edges by big white pines mixed in with scrubby jacks. Generally, the few houses that were nearby looked like ours. Not much to look at, but neat and taken care of. A sandy driveway connected to the road in front. No grass to speak of around the house. Whatever was there was what nature provided. Near the corner of where the driveway and road met stood a rickety old mailbox anchored in a cinder block. The driveway actually was another, bigger sandy place for me to play. We had no car. Thank God every place we needed to go was within walking distance. That was okay on the good days, but rainy days and winter were a challenge.

There was a small garden on the side of the house. Between that and the corner of the house was my little sandbox. Mom had her clothesline near there, between the garden and the toilet. *Did you know you could actually break the frozen sheets hanging there in the winter? Well, I found out. Not a good thing.*

Back to the toilet—everybody had one then. Three holes and a trough it was, with a Sears catalog hanging on the wall next to the door and within easy reach. *Yup, toilet paper. No quilted Charmin for us. Hint: stay away from those glossy pages—they hurt.* I always wondered why there were so many holes when all you needed was one at a time. Unless you expected company! Typically, one doesn't regard an outhouse as a source of much entertainment, but this one was destined to provide me with one heck of an unforgettable memory.

One warm day, while I was sitting there waiting for nature to do its thing, I occupied my time with the only toy I had—a little red truck given to me by one of the neighbors. Kind of beat-up and with chipped paint, but to me it was brand-new. It had well-worn tires and a little fake steering wheel inside. I loved it. I took it everywhere I went. So there I sat—rolling it back and forth to pass the time. But I stopped playing and concentrated on the reason I was there, and placed my truck next to me on the left. There must have been some magical attraction on my truck by that huge hole next to me. By the time I saw it move it was too late. Down it went! Through that big hole. Now, apparently the bench with all those holes I was sitting on had a slight tilt from the back wall of the toilet to the front edge. It was hardly noticeable, but it was there, although I didn't know it. God, I didn't know what to do. I finished what nature had sent me to do and looked down into that horrible place. My truck was hung up on a support beam directly below and about four feet down. I couldn't reach it.

I was in a serious and odoriferous situation, to say the least. I had to figure out how to retrieve my only toy from the gate to hell where I had placed it. I finally gained a critical understanding—an "Aha!" moment. I suddenly knew the reason for the extra holes. ***They eat toys!*** Apparently, they were put in places like these to control the ever-expanding toy population. At least that was the view of this four-year-old. I wondered how many other toys were lost due to unnecessary holes that thrived on eating toys. I didn't know what was worse—the boogeyman in the cellar or a toy-eating toilet hole!

It is amazing how valuable something can be when there is nothing to replace it. What to do?

I got up enough courage to fess up to Mom. She went out immediately to assess the situation. I could tell by the look on her face she was not pleased. Like she had nothing else to do!

"What did you do that for?" she asked, as if I planned the entire kidnapping.

"I didn't do it, it was an accident. That big hole ate it," I said unconvincingly.

With a disdainful frown on her face she cried out for my older sister, who was sitting in the rope swing across the yard. "Go get that rope over by the clothesline and bring it to me."

Sis found the rope and brought it to Mom, dropping it next to the toilet door. Why Mom needed the rope was confusing to her—but not for long! She began to return to what she had been doing, when Mom stopped her and said, "Hold on, I need your help. Come over here and turn around." Mom fashioned a loop from the rope and slipped it over Sis's head and under her arms.

"What are you doing, Mom?" Sis asked, as if already knowing what was in store.

"Your brother dropped his toy down the toilet. I am going to lower you down this hole and I want you to grab your brother's truck sitting on the beam just below. Do you see it?"

Oh, the expression on my sister's face was a masterpiece of horror. I also thought Mom had wrongfully blamed me for that toy-eating hole in there. I withstood the pain of being blamed.

"Mom! You want me to do what?" she said, in serious disbelief. "Do you know what's down there? Besides, it stinks down there!"

"Yes, your brother's toy. It's the only one he's got and I can't afford another. Now, please stand still while I put this around you. Don't worry, you'll be fine." I don't think Sis was referring to the toy when she pointed out what was down there.

My sister had shock written all over her face. Needless to say, my reasonably warm relationship with my sister was now at risk of sudden death.

"I hope you're happy," she said with a sneer, looking at me with hate-filled eyes and communicating a side of her I had never seen before.

She very reluctantly did as she was told, however. Mom raised her up and lowered her down. I could hear her griping about the terrible violation of her otherwise calm and peaceful day—all because of me and that villainous and unnecessary hole in the toilet created by very evil people for the purpose of eating toys. Go figure!

After a short while she grabbed it and yelled to Mom to raise her up. Immediately after, both it and she were given a very thorough bath. When she became approachable I gave her a big hug while holding on to my now clean and uniquely christened truck. "Thanks, Sis," was all I could come up with.

We had won the battle of the toilet hole, and Sis's standing with me was elevated to that of a superhero— and I told her so. Now we had to invent a name for our new superhero. I tried to think of what would fit. Hmm…

Over the years, I often wondered if, had the situation been reversed, I would have been as obedient. I was, however, extremely grateful to her. Now that I knew the reason for the other holes I would never allow them to eat any more of my toys. *Sis even got an extra bath that week!*

TWO

Time passes
New things happening
Changes for all
It was good

Despite the hardship we suffered during the many years alone without a dad, we never gave up. Especially Mom! Looking back, I know it was Mom that made survival possible. It wasn't all bad, though—no more fighting or worries for Mom about the attacks after the heavy drinking at the bars. Being abandoned by Dad was bad, but at the same time things were far better now, considering the cleansed atmosphere around the house because of his absence.

I didn't know what I was missing having just one parent, which was normal for me. All of my friends had a dad, but I never gave it much thought. Dad left before I could know him, so it was impossible for me to know what having a dad meant. Nor were there any really good examples of a male figure in my life at that time. No dad to show me the guy things. No big dad person to toss me into the air and play games with. I had no idea of how important a committed dad was for children during those early years until I became one.

Divorce was accomplished in absentia, or without Dad present, in 1949. He wasn't around to defend himself of the legal actions taken. Now Mom was free to move on. And she did! To earn much-needed money, Mom continued to take in the soldiers' laundry and wait tables at one of the local restaurants. Neighbors would help with baby-sitting when needed.

Suitors for her appeared now and then. One of them was named Al. He was a chiropractor and I must say quite stuffy. He always dressed like he either just came from church or was about to go there, albeit the clothes were virtually colorless, drab, and somewhat loose and ill-fitting. He always wore a tie, too.

"What the heck is a chiropractor?" I asked, hardly able to pronounce the word. He stared down at me with a grimace, which gave me the distinct impression that I had just asked a very dumb question.

"I'm a doctor and adjust people's bones," he said impatiently. Well, let me tell you, I was not sure just how to take that response. Hmm. Adjusting people's bones had to be a pretty hard thing to do. It had to hurt, too! Frankenstein-like images of horror suddenly started popping into my head. I didn't want to know more. Boris Karloff had some competition!

Al must have been pretty serious about Mom because one day he took all of us to Milwaukee to meet his parents. We had to get gussied up and there were strict orders about good behavior. I remember being stuffed like sardines in his nice new Studebaker car. Al was constantly talking about his new car. It had one of those new things called an automatic. Automatic what, I didn't grasp, but it was an automatic. Whatever it was, it made it really special. I could tell from the pride in its owner—the chiropractor.

Al was edgy with the three of us kids in the back—apparently wondering if we were going to throw up on his nice new seats or do something equally unpleasant.

He kept looking at us in the mirror with hard discerning stares. Once in a while he would glance over to Mom and smile, giving him a more human quality.

It was a long ride, but we finally got to his parents' home not far from downtown. Nice folks, friendly. His dad took me to the zoo. I had never seen things like that before. Even rode on a streetcar. They're long gone now. Too bad, 'cause they are fun, especially for a five-year-old.

I couldn't figure out how such nice people could have had a kid who grew up and turned into a torturous, bone-adjusting doctor with zero personality. But they did. We told Mom we didn't like him very much.

Soon Al was a thing of the past. I do not know to this day if Al went away because he and Mom didn't quite make it or if it was due to the fact that I was a dumb kid who asked him what a bone doctor was. Or maybe it was that hex one of my sisters put on him. Didn't care, 'cause he was history.

But that was Al number one. Al number two was next. I guess Al was a pretty popular name for guys back then. Either that or Mom had a serious disabling fetish for guys named Al.

Al number two was a skinny kid-like guy. He seemed too young to want to go with my much-older-looking mom. He was from the Army fort nearby. Yup, Mom did his laundry, too. Maybe that was the draw, free laundry service. Nevertheless, he kept showing up at our place, usually late in the day and always hungry. I didn't think this one would go as far with Mom as did Al number one. It didn't. There were a few others, but none of them rang any bells for Mom—or us—except one.

One day a new guy showed up. Nope—his name wasn't Al. Now that was a serious move in the right direction! Apparently, Mom and this guy were seeing each other at the restaurant where Mom waited tables. She hadn't mentioned him before, so we were taken aback a bit when he came into the picture. He drove a truck for a big car manufacturer. Hmm! A truck driver! Not a chiropractor. Again we were making progress. He was what I wanted to be—a truck driver. He passed the first test!

I could tell something was happening. Mom seemed to be continually fluttering about, even singing once in a while and she can't sing. She also would take longer to ready herself for work. Got very picky about girl stuff.

This went on for several months. Then one day Mom said we all had to be on our best behavior because we were going to have company. She had asked him over to meet us, ostensibly to test or shock him with the clear and present danger of being in the presence of three impish kids.

Later that day he showed up. He drove up in this really odd-looking old car. An old Ford coupe is what he called it. Black as the ace of spades and hardly any room inside. No backseat. But that didn't matter; we weren't planning a trip to Milwaukee.

Tall dude, too! Not heavy, but looked strong. Well built, I would say. He had blond hair as far as I could tell. It was very short, in the style called a flat top. He had on what I guessed were his work clothes, khaki pants and a matching tan shirt.

Mom saw him drive up and met him at the door. They both were wearing broad grins. I could tell they sort of liked each other. Both sisters were eager to meet him and did. I was shy and held back. Mom called for me to come meet him, but I was not quite ready for that. Just then, he sought me out from across the room and approached.

Kneeling down, he said, "Well now, who do we have here? What's your name, Bub?" I was acting shy and turned away to hide my face in the corner of the walls. I knew one thing for sure—he didn't know my name, 'cause it sure wasn't Bub.

Something was different with this guy, besides not having a first name of Al. I actually started to like him. He was twenty-six and fairly attractive. Mom was a bit older but they made a good pair. I wasn't sure where all this was going. He kept coming around. Apparently, the thought of three impish kids didn't scare him away. He passed the second test. But there would be others.

Mom finally confessed to the three of us that she had found someone she could and did love and wanted to marry. Yup, she was hooked. I would imagine he sort of felt the same way. One major consideration for this to happen was that he had to pass the test of the three children who would be part of the deal. It appeared he was okay with that.

He had never been married before. Now, I had to ask, who had the greater adjustment to make, him or us? How many men would jump into a marriage with a woman and a ready-made family in absolute destitution? Either he was surely out of his mind or he was so in lust with Mom that it didn't matter. Hmm!

I really didn't know how all this was going to happen. Seemingly, all of a sudden things began to change around the place. We were going to get a dad. How does that work? Changes were in the works. He came by a lot, practically living with us. Slowly, we were getting used to this guy. He was clearly different from the others. He actually took an interest in us, although when he did we were filled with suspicion that he was doing it to impress us—and more importantly, Mom. Did he really understand we were part of the deal? We had a lot of doubts. Little by little, though, the doubts diminished and trust grew. Questions continued for a long time, though, about how he would fit in. How do you get a new parent and where do you stick that person in the chain?

Below all the emotion of these pending changes I began to like the idea. I began to like him. We were becoming friends. On that special day, we three were shoved off to the house of one of the neighbors while Mom and our new dad-to-be went off in his little coupe with no backseat.

Later on that day I saw them drive up. I was convinced the deed had been done. I ran up to the driver's side and looked him square in the eyes. He rolled the window down and smiled. Mom was all dressed up and sitting on the other side with a silly-looking grin from ear to ear. She was different today.

"Are you my daddy yet?" I asked.

"Not yet, Bub, but soon," he replied. There was that name again. I was sure by now that he was smart enough to remember my name. He was most certainly confused. It occurred to me that once they tied the knot I might be getting a new first name. I wasn't sure where this was going. I let it pass.

He became our new dad and it was good. There were tons of things to get used to—for all of us. He finally learned my name and admitted that he called all little guys that name. Well, if I were to be his son he had to learn my name—he agreed and did.

They had been married for nearly two years already. We were now well settled into our new family arrangement.

One day, however, a strange lady visited. It was a summer afternoon in 1954. Mom introduced to her as a person from a government organization. She wanted to talk to all three of us kids. We were instructed to go into the bedroom and sit on the edge of the bed, and the lady would be in soon. That was the only room where there could be any privacy, and we were to talk to this lady without Mom and our new daddy there. I was confused and a bit nervous, even though I was the ripe old age of almost eight. What was happening?

"Hello, children, I'm Mrs. Stone. I'm from the welfare office," she said. I thought that name was a suitable name, considering the look on her face—it matched. Reminded me of one of the teachers we had been subjected to last term. Yuck! Her demeanor was professional, but I had no idea what the welfare office was. She wore a light blue businesslike dress with an open white V-collar. She had on an overdose of some awful perfume that matched the overdone deep red lipstick. All that competed with the somewhat conservative hairdo: dark mixed with gray strands, shoulder length and straight!

"I am here to talk to you three about your new daddy," she said, with a forced smile. I thought she must have been as nervous as we were because I could see a small twitch in her right cheek.

"Do you like your new daddy?" she asked each of us, one at a time. My older sister pondered a moment but responded in the affirmative. Then she got to me. Although I did like my new daddy, I was very curious about what would happen to him if I said no. We were suddenly empowered. It was us over the adults—and apparently we were being given control. How often did that happen?

"Yup," I said smugly. "He's nice. Why do you want to know?"

"Well, I am here because your mom and dad have decided to have you three adopted by him," she replied.

Now I knew the adults had pulled a fast one. We weren't empowered after all. They were preparing us for this thing they called "adopted." What the hell was that? It was a setup!

"What's 'adopted' mean?" I asked. My sisters gave me a look as if I had just emerged from some aboriginal cave, but I was sure they didn't know, either. I let it go.

"Well, it is a complicated matter. First, right now your dad really isn't your daddy. He is more what is called a 'foster parent.' He is your mom's husband but not your daddy—legally," she said.

God, now I knew I had opened a seriously big can of worms. "Not legally our daddy," she had said. So maybe he was "illegally" our daddy, I thought. What a mess! Grown-ups sure knew how to complicate things.

She went on. "Your daddy has a different last name than you do, and he and your mom want you to have his last name." Until that time I had never really given much thought to last names. I didn't care.

"Would you like to have a new last name?" she asked. The three of us just sat there. For the first time in memory my sisters were speechless. That was a cherished moment for me.

"How do you spell it?" I asked. I had to show how smart I was, so I had to sort of challenge the subject, even though the inevitable was likely going to happen. She spelled his name. Hmm, only eight letters compared to my nine. It sounded good, too.

"Okay," I said. "What happens next?"

"Nothing for you, dear," she said. "I have some forms to fill out, and I will recommend that we proceed with the adoption process." I remember bragging to all my friends that I had a new last name. They didn't believe me, but that was okay.

After the private meeting was over, we all went into the other room where Mom and our new dad were waiting.

"Well, what did you say to her?" Dad asked.

"I told her I wasn't happy and didn't want to change my name," I said. Although I was joking, I could tell for a split second that he was thinking I meant it.

"Just kidding," I said, then went over and gave him a big hug. *I have a dad, just like all the rest of the kids*, I thought.

Boy, things are sure complicated. Little did I know that this process would sever any possible legal connection with my real dad. If I had known that, I am sure to this day that I still would have said yes. As it turned out, in the far distant future my old last name would come back to haunt me. I would later discover that I had two half sisters and a half brother that I came to love dearly. How we met is another story, but just know that neither of my grandmothers nor anyone else talked about the actions of my biological father. It was as if that part of my life was wiped clean. Taboo to discuss, too!

THREE

Those wonder years
Full of extremes

I lay there thinking. Not much else to do when you're alone and waiting. Waiting till tomorrow. The operation was scheduled for then. But there I was, checked in, in bed, wearing nothing but a smock open in the back. I supposed having an opening in the ass area had some meaning, but all I knew was it wasn't comfortable—kinda breezy.

My thoughts went back to some early day high points, mostly in school. I didn't like school much, which was evident on my report cards. I was and am a dreamer. I knew I was smart and didn't think I had to prove it to anyone. Typical of most kids, I suppose. From those early days of the sandbox to sitting in the swing affixed between two tall white pine trees in the backyard, I was alone. Always alone in my world. Same was true in the classroom.

It was a sudden shock to me when my fourth grade teacher conspired with Mom to discuss keeping me back a grade. My scholastic rebellion had to come to an end, but I had issues. My reading was off, my arithmetic didn't make sense, and in general I was behind. I threw a fit and begged not to be kept back. They agreed, but I had to earn their trust by doing self-study during the summer months, and if I failed, off I would go in the fall to repeat the last year. The threats of being held back hurt; I didn't want to be mixed with those lower-class stooges. That thought alone was enough of a kick to get me going. And it worked! But liking school had nothing to do with learning. It was much more...

It was in the sixth grade that I found a better reason to go to school. Her name was Gloria. Every day this cute little kid from two grades down would do everything in her power to get me to notice her.

One day while sitting in class I was nudged by a buddy, who pointed to the window of the room door. It was her, winking at me. Who was she? My buddy said she was looking at me. At me? What was going on? I later learned she had the hots for me. One might ponder how any fourth grader would have the hots for anyone. This cute kid did. I was in her trap—and I liked it! My first crush—wow!

It didn't take me long to begin checking her out. She was cute and seemed older than her age. I divulged my deepest crush for this girl to only my most trusted friends. She was two grades below. Then again, I was very young for my age, which I thought was a key rationalization and leveling point. We would meet on the playground, secluding ourselves as best we could from the others so we wouldn't get teased.

Our local radio station would play all the tunes we liked and take dedications from school kids between three and five o'clock every weekday. Being in love like I was, I wanted to impress Gloria so I called and requested Elvis's "Love Me Tender." Bill at the radio station was happy to oblige. It was a surprise for Gloria so I didn't tell her, but I knew she liked to listen a lot during those hours.

I couldn't wait until the next day to see her face, knowing the most popular song of all time was dedicated to us. So there I was, glued to the radio—and then it came.

"This next song is dedicated to Gloria from her love," he said, and he named me. I waited anxiously and then it started to play. My heart pounding, I listened. Wait—they got it WRONG! I was expecting "Love Me Tender" and got "Tom Dooley"! What the hell was that all about? From one of the most sensitive, loving songs to a song of a guy about to meet his maker hanging from a tree. My love life was over. I wanted to hide in a hole somewhere. How could I face her or any of my classmates tomorrow? Somehow, I found enough courage to deal with whatever would come my way. I could not think of an excuse Mom would buy to allow me to stay home, so I was stuck.

As I entered the school and looked around for her, I was approached by several of my friends. *This was it*, I thought. *It's over now.* Huh! There was no mention of it. What? Didn't they listen to the radio? Guess not. I then saw Gloria down the hall—our eyes met. I had just enough time before the bell, so I ran to her as fast as I could, sure that she would not want to talk to me because of a guy named Tom Dooley. I was wrong. I didn't say a word about the song and neither did she. Was I saved? Yes! No one in my world, including Gloria, had heard the broadcast. There was a GOD!

Now, in the hospital, I laughed out loud and sprang myself out of my daydream, but continued thinking of her. I wondered where Gloria was now and if she ever thought about us and those times of seemingly a lifetime ago. Did she remember the times we would sneak to the movies to see each other, or how I would steal a kiss from her on the playground whenever I could? I never did tell her about that guy named Tom Dooley.

Suddenly, my attention was drawn from the window of my darkening room and watching the late-afternoon bustle of the street below to the door to my room. A slight knock and then the door opened slowly. She was holding a small tray in her left hand. She was dressed in a uniform of some kind; it had pink stripes running up and down against white linen-like fabric, but the uniform wasn't a nurse's. On the one hand, it was startling to have an intrusion in the quiet of my reminiscing, but on the other hand it would be nice to have someone to talk to—even for a short time. I had been there for several hours and the thought of the next day was on my mind, I welcomed anything that would take my mind off the operation.

As she approached my bed I could only concentrate on how pretty she was. She was young, but I wasn't sure how young. Her straight, shoulder-length hair was dark brown—almost black. Her sparkling dark brown eyes were penetrating and beautiful. She had little dimples on both cheeks that coupled with her cute smile.

"Hello, there, how are you doing?" she asked.

"Fine," I said, wondering who she was and why I was so lucky to get such a pretty visitor. "What do you have there?" I asked.

"Oh, this? Just something to brighten your day. Just some juice and some candy mints." She came over and set the little tray on the larger one next to my bed. "What are you here for?"

"Surgery in the morning," I said. "I have a cyst on my spine. Nothing too serious, but it requires the knife."

"Oh, that sounds pretty serious to me, though. What time is your surgery?"

"Seven is what they told me," I replied. "Are you a nurse or something?"

"Oh, no—just an aide, sort of. I want to be someday, though." She was about to leave, but suddenly turned around and said, "Good luck with your operation. I'll stop by tomorrow and see how you're doing."

She left and the room seemed so empty all of a sudden. The lights outside dimmed more as the day wore on. The chime of the clock on the bank across the street rang out the hour—you always knew the time of day. I was hungry, too! No food for me, though—just liquids, they told me. They apparently had to starve the patient in order to understand relative pain—the pangs of hunger or the pain of the knife. I sucked on one of those magic mints that girl had placed on my tray. It helped a little, but more than that, it caused me to think of how pretty that girl was. I couldn't wait to see her again. Thinking of her made waiting for surgery a lot easier.

It was still night when the door suddenly swung open. "Good morning," a nurse said loudly. "And how are we doing this morning?" It must have been around five—the clock chime of the bank across the street evidently didn't ring during the night. I wasn't sure how to respond to her query. I was doing fine, but wasn't sure why she wanted to include herself in her question.

"I'm fine, I guess," I replied. "What's that?" I asked, referring to a tray with a long needle on it.

"This is for you, it will help make you relax," she said. "It's called a hypo. Now relax and roll over on your side."

I did as she told me. She uncovered my now fully exposed naked butt. She took the long needle and gave it to me in the right butt cheek. It didn't hurt much. "The doctor will be in soon to talk to you about what he will be doing during your surgery," she said. "Now just relax, it will be over soon."

The doctor came in just as she said and explained the high points of the pending operation. He didn't stay long. "See you in a little while," he said. It was all business and quick.

A little later, a man came in with a cart and slid me onto it and off we went. The passing lights on the ceiling were almost hypnotic as we moved down the hall. Made me dizzy watching—obviously, the shot was starting to work. It was cold in the hallway—but then, I really had nothing on under the thin blanket except the short smock they had issued me when I checked in, which was fully open in the rear.

Into the elevator and down to surgery we went. The room was extremely bright—and cold, too. Next, they removed the smock, and now there I was with nothing but a sheet covering my otherwise naked sixteen-year-old body.

The hypo was working now. My head was spinning, but not enough to prevent me from noticing a classmate of mine doing something with the instruments off in the corner of the room—sterilizing them, I think. *What's she doing here?* I thought. *What is Mary doing HERE!* I was drugged, but was sure I was completely aware. She looked over at me and smiled at the same time the nurse was moving me onto the operating table. I was totally naked and about to flash one of my classmates. And that was exactly what happened! No one seemed to care except me. I said nothing. I tried to be cool, like this was something I did every day, but this was the first time I had ever been naked in front of a girl. I later learned that Mary worked part-time in the surgical ward and operating room taking care of the equipment. She never said anything when I returned to school, but I'll never forget being naked in front of her. Believe me, this was not a sexual event! The next thing I noticed was the doctor in full surgical garb instructing the anesthesiologist to go ahead. In a flash I was out!

When I woke up I had this overpowering pain in my buttocks. It was easy to guess that I had been under the knife and seriously violated. I couldn't lie on my back because of the excessive bandages and the pain in my ass. I was slowly coming around. The taste of whatever they had used in surgery was lingering. Yuck! I felt queasy because of it. So there I was; maimed and feeling very much helpless. The operation was a success, per the doctor's statement while I was in post-op recovery. I could tell he was seriously surer of the success than I was. The big difference was that it was my ass that hurt—not his! I remember thinking how amazing it was that we find ourselves trusting others with all we have. He had a degree from some school, which was supposed to guarantee my trust. Hell, what else was I going to do? But because I trusted him I was stuck with a sore in my butt and sick to my stomach. For a guy, that is very disarming and not too macho.

A little later I was moved back to my room. I was told I would be able to go home in a couple of days.

I wasn't sure about that from the amount of pain in my ass.

I lay there thinking of anything I could to keep from wondering what my ass looked like. If it looked as bad as it felt I would clearly be in trouble. I wondered, though, if that beautiful young aide would come by like she said. I hoped so!

I didn't have to wait long before the door quietly opened. Ah, it was her. The grin on my face was an obvious welcome sign for her. This time she didn't bring anything, but came right over to the bedside.

"Hi, there," she said. "I checked the roster and saw that you were out of recovery and moved back. My name is Pam. I work a few hours a week as an aide. I was thinking of you a lot today. How do you feel?" She really sounded concerned and that made me feel a quantum leap better.

Suddenly, I was no longer feeling the pain in my back side. Somehow, the charge of hormone-driven adrenaline of a sixteen-year-old boy in the presence of a beautiful girl erased all of that. After a rather lengthy introduction from each of us, I knew her name, her age—nineteen—and that her uncle was one of the doctors there. We managed a weak promise to see each other after I was out of the hospital. *That,* I thought, *would be too good to be true.* Surely, a girl who looked like her certainly would be not interested in a kid three years younger. But there was always hope. She was cheating on the clock to come and see me, so we had to compress the communication as best we could. Maybe she really was interested in me. She said she had to leave, but as she approached the door she turned and said she would be back tomorrow. And then she said something that sealed my love life for all eternity.

"You're cute," she said, and left the room wearing a smile and showing off those dimples.

Hearing that was too much—I was soaring high. I was speechless. Needless to say, my mind was far off the pain in my butt. I had met the girl of my dreams! Having an operation was the only way to go! This turn of events gave going to the hospital a whole different meaning.

The next couple of days were heavenly, with Pam visiting every time she could—sometimes several times in less than a few hours. Wow! What a dream! When Mom and Dad came by for a short visit they couldn't understand my happy-go-lucky attitude. I could tell they were happy with the improvement, whatever the cause. I didn't mention Pam. It just took the right kind of motivation. Things were happening fast. Not only did I get my back side taken care of, but I learned of a whole new world. I was in love.

There never was any serious physical contact in that room, but a whole lot of hand-holding and a kiss whenever we felt brave enough. We strengthened the vow we had taken earlier to be together after I was out. We kept the promise. She was nineteen and I was sixteen. I didn't care if she was an older woman. She was wonderful.

She and I would do everything we could to get to see each other. She lived about three miles from me on the other side of the river. On good weather days, Pam would either find a way to come by the house or I would do whatever I could to be with her at her home. We would do what every overly excited teenager would do. For the record—we didn't do THAT! Just a lot of petting and talk. Oh, make no mistake, I wanted more! And from all indications so did Pam.

One day Pam suggested we go to my room to have a look at some of my models (rockets and airplanes). Yeah, right! Mom and Dad were working and the sisters were gone somewhere. We were alone, as was typical whenever she came by. After we entered the room she sat down on the edge of my bed.

"Wanna come sit by me?" she asked. I slowly went over and sat next to her, and could sense that I was about to be tested. I actually began to get nervous, a little. Sorta scared, too. I was floating; my head started to spin. Oh my God!

Then she leaned over and gave me a big French kiss. I was immediately propelled into space giving Alan Shepard some serious competition. He needed a spaceship. I didn't!

"Um, what are we doing?" I asked stupidly, knowing exactly where this could go. She didn't say anything and just looked deeply into my eyes. I could feel the maleness in me, which was far ahead of my readiness.

"I thought you wanted to," she finally responded. Now, how would any normal all-American boy NOT want it? It was scary. Although I wanted it more than just about anything, I couldn't go through with it. I felt so not in control—but at the same time, I felt very mature. She wanted me! I had never felt that way before.

Somehow, in the next few moments I regained my earthly foundation and realized I was indeed in trouble. What to do! If I said no I would possibly lose her and if I said yes I would definitely lose ME. It was the most difficult thing, but I chose the former.

"I love you, Pam, and want to, but I can't go through with it," I said, after a slight pause.

I was now positive she thought I was queer or something. After all, every male has only one thing on his mind, and in that regard I was absolutely NORMAL, but my response to her was not that type of normal. Things were happening so fast.

She was ready, but I wasn't—I was scared. As much as I wanted it, and to be able to smugly flaunt my conquest to my closest friends, I just couldn't go through with it. I was sure, however, that she would leave me and tell everyone what a wimp I was. She didn't.

She wanted a man and I was still a boy, a scared one. But we remained friends, just friends. I moved on, thinking that I had given up one of the best opportunities a man could have. I didn't. Hmm, we never did look at my models in my room, either—go figure!

Pam moved on and likely discovered more willing lovers, and I was sure I was saved from early fatherhood by some divine force. My future remained safe—so far.

It was a short-lived romance, but I'll never forget the time when I went to the hospital, flashed a classmate, and got a pain in both my ass and my heart at the same time.

FOUR

Early challenges
Meeting them head-on
Choosing a direction

It was the challenge of school and I remember...

It was the waning days of high school—my senior year, the only year I actually applied myself. The days of Pam and others were over and now I had to deal with me and where I was to fit in the tomorrows ahead. Where was I going? My first thoughts on the subject were those which generally caused fear—and, I might add, a bit of anger. I was anxious to move on. I wanted out of this small town—a normal feeling for a teen.

My scholastic performance was seriously lacking, although I knew I was much more talented than the grades indicated. Yeah, I bet everyone says that! Well, in my case it was true. I hated most aspects of school. I had my favorite subjects, but couldn't prove it with my slightly above average grades in those areas.

I had good teachers there, too, but sometimes their truthfulness was extremely hard to swallow. Considering my future, I had conversations with both my math and physics teachers. Although nice enough in their counsel, I was left empty when both provided me guidance in such a way that one could be sure they had rehearsed the same response before I met with them.

"So, you have had a good year. And now what do you want to do?" said the math teacher.

"I don't know. I was thinking of joining the military, but my parents are not supportive, and since I won't be eighteen until late in the year, I have to do something. They want me to go on in school someplace," I said, wondering if I was boring him.

"Well, going on in school is a wonderful idea. I would suggest a vocational school, but definitely not college. Unfortunately, your performance is not quite to that level. If you do try, you really should stay away from the hard sciences and mathematical areas. You had a fair run this past year, but I do not believe you are strong enough in either to suggest a go at it," he said.

I could tell he meant well and didn't want to hurt my feelings. To be honest, I hadn't given going to college any thought, so in that regard I was okay with what he said. Thank God this was a private conversation, though—I didn't need to have any classmates hearing what a dummy I was.

I was again beat down, likely due to my dreamer attitude throughout my educational path. The enemy was me and the fault mine.

I went home that day feeling down and thinking I was trapped. I explained to my mom what both teachers had said. She didn't respond, except to say that she still was unwilling to sign for me to join up. It was 1964 and the Vietnam War was raging, with no sign of a letup. I truly didn't care whether it was or wasn't; I wanted to get out and be on my own, but I couldn't.

The very day after graduation we moved on to another town two hours away because Dad had a new job there. It was a town about ten times bigger than home. It had educational opportunities and I found a place to go.

Ultimately, I did follow the teacher's advice and entered a vocational school, taking up electronics repair. I ended up working part-time as a stock boy at a local discount store during the day. The other students in the class were nice people, all males, and old enough to be my dad. I couldn't fault them for wanting to improve their lives with an electronics repair certificate, but for me there had to be more. I was getting straight A's but not liking it. I couldn't wait till birthday number eighteen arrived. I was going to get out then, for sure. Until one day while on a break my boss came over to me and said something that would change my life.

"Hey, what ya going to do with yourself?" he asked. "I mean, you can't be a stock boy forever." He was right. I explained to him my dilemma with both my youth and the school I was attending.

"Why do you care?" I asked, trying not to sound too inconsiderate.

"Because I was in your spot once and I see myself all over again just watching you. I got stuck along the way. I struggled and made it this far in my career, but this job, although much better than where you are at, doesn't pay enough for me to support a family. So, to make a long story short, I am enrolled at the UW–Whitewater and am studying something that will, with a degree, let me move out of this rut." He continued to tell me that he wanted to get married but couldn't afford it.

"Well, I appreciate what you are saying, but there ain't much I can do about it," I said.

"That's not necessarily true," he said. "Come with me tomorrow. I have to go over to the school to pre-register for the fall. You may find some things there that would interest you."

"Well, you're the boss. Sure, I'll come. What time?"

"I'll come by around eight—plan on a whole day."

As we approached the school I could make out the bell tower of Old Main. It was a school which started as a normal school in 1868—a teacher's school. It was still primarily a school for teachers, but now offered many other major studies. I followed my boss around getting a feel for the place. It was summer so not much activity was going on. We stopped by an office where I was given a catalog of academics. The people at the office asked if I was interesting in enrolling.

"Oh, no," I replied. "I can't."

"Well, if it's money, we have programs you may be interested in," she said. She actually sounded like she would earn recruiting points and was trying hard to get me to sign up. I was taken, however, by what she said. I didn't have the courage to tell her I was not up to college level. Finally, I asked if she had any information on what was required to enter, besides money. She explained that the school required certain levels on the SAT test, but if the scores were lower than that they had a program to enter the student on academic probation. After that, if you didn't make the minimum grades—you're out! I finally got up enough courage to explain my scholastic standing dilemma. She understood.

"Here," she said. "Take these forms with you, along with the catalog. Go home and discuss it with your parents. Who knows, you just might be a student here in the fall."

My head was flying high. I felt a pang deep inside me, but I didn't know its source. I suddenly felt that maybe, just maybe, I might have a chance to do something that would alter my life for the good—and for forever.

"So, what did that lady tell you when I left you there this morning?" asked my boss. We were on our way back home, and while in the car all I could think of was my encounter with that nice lady in the registrar's office.

"Well, she sort of tried to recruit me, I guess."

"You didn't see me, but I was about to enter the office during your conversation and held back because I saw the light in your eyes as you listened to her. You're hooked," he said. "Did she give you anything?"

"Yeah, an application, a book, and a smile," I said.

"Think it over, but remember, if you want to go to this school you should get on the paperwork now!" he said. "I think the store manager would give you all the slack you need regarding your schedule and any part-time work in the future. He is a believer in helping the youth out."

"Thanks. I need to talk to my parents."

I did just that. Mom was very supportive. Dad wasn't. His attitude took me by surprise. He thought I should move out as soon as I was old enough, like he did when he was young. Well, he was drafted into World War II. But I could tell he saw this opportunity as a never-ending drain on his wallet—at least that was the impression I got.

Mom and Dad had it out over this. In fact, the argument was so huge I actually took some of my belongings and left, slamming the door behind me so hard the neighbors could definitely pick up on the row. I had tears in my eyes as I yelled back at them, "Forget the whole damned thing! I don't need your help! Or your permission!" I actually had no place to go. I just went out the door and didn't look back. I must have gone a few blocks down the street when I came to the realization that I was again treed—up a tree without a ladder. No place to go except back to that inferno of a home. So that was what I did—after I made sure I had waited long enough to give them both time to think I might have really gone somewhere. I had to have them trapped at least a little.

Sheepishly, I entered the house through the rear door. They had stopped the argument and once again peace, or at least a truce, was in place. I hated it when they fought. It always made me think back to the earliest days when I used to hear my original Dad and Mom fight.

Apparently Mom had won. Dad just looked at me and sort of half smiled. He did explain why he had come across the way he did. It wasn't the money thing, it was his attitude that a man needs to get out of the house as soon as possible. *He never had a chance to go on to school. In fact, Dad had been held back in school in his early years and was already eighteen when he was a junior. World War II was raging at the time and the draft board picked him. Had he been the same age and in his senior year, they would have given him a chance to finish. So, he had no high school diploma.* Mom had convinced him that he was out of line and he seemingly accepted his defeat. I was going to apply. Eventually Dad got used to the idea.

I had to hurry; all the forms had to be filled out and the transcripts sent. Weeks later I received a letter from the school indicating that I was accepted as a student, but on academic probation. I had to maintain a minimum of a 2.0 GPA or I would be an ex-student. I was both elated and scared at the same time. I was assured by my parents, and especially Dad, with the old adage of "nothing ventured, nothing gained."

There was a mandatory meeting at the school prior to the start of the fall semester. It was for all students. There must have been thousands there, making me even more acutely nervous. We formed up in the football field bleachers. Way down in the middle and behind a microphone stood the dean of students.

"Welcome to Whitewater," he began. He continued with an introductory speech confirming his welcome for us. "Look to either side of you and remember their faces," he said. "Four years from now those two faces will be gone." Obviously, math wasn't his strong point. His algorithm, if really applied, would mean we all would be gone. His point was understood, however, that two out of three would not make it to graduation.

I did, however, remember those faces on either side. Yup, they were gone four years later—but I WASN'T! Hmm, maybe the ole dean did have some math expertise after all. Oh, well, I made it. I never did find out what happened to the others; realizing, of course, that their absence did nothing to secure my success.

Later that same day we had more forms to fill out. We were instructed to declare a major and a minor course of study. I had never given any thought to a major or a minor, so I asked around and got little or no advice. A girl next to me suggested picking whatever I liked and said not to worry about it, I could always change it later. So I did: major—chemistry, minor—mathematics! As I did, I could hear the spirit-like voices of my high school teachers echoing their disagreement with my choices. I had committed a sin against all logical forces or something. What else could I do? I was only interested in those areas. Little did I know then that my course of study was going to be a four-year kick in the ass. I would live to see that it was worth all the pain.

So, time leaped forward. My grades in school were good, and in some cases better than good. I was not blessed with valedictorian or salutatorian standing, but I held my own. The social pressures were extreme but all part of the education.

It was my senior year of college and the spring semester was fast approaching. It had been nearly four years since I started this trek. I was ready to graduate—except for one thing. I needed fourteen more credits to meet the minimum number required for graduation. I had figure out something. I hated the space-filling and non-educational courses—I wanted something I could use, something I knew I would like. I decided to request permission for a double major. I consulted my professors in both the chemistry and mathematics departments. I asked their opinion on the possibility of a double major: chemistry and mathematics. They said I could do it, but it would not be fun. They both cautiously gave me the approving nod, but advised that I would need the approval of both department chairs. I heeded their counsel and got the approval. They all looked at me like I was some masochistic psychotic idiot, though; as if to say, what in hell would any NORMAL student do this for—a double major declaration in the final semester of school. The weather was getting warm, and pre-graduation parties were planned and happening already for the soon-to-be-graduated senior class. What was I doing while the parties were going on? Studying my ass off, trapped in the dorm thinking how stupid I must be to have done that to myself. But I went ahead and did it anyway.

One course in particular was giving me serious difficulty: topology. It was a course I needed to complete and had to do so with reasonably honorable grade in math in order for me not only to have a double major but to graduate on time. Our grades were dependent on class participation, homework, and midterm and final projects. I got the class participation and homework okay, but the kickers were the projects. I slid by the midterm in reasonable shape but the final exam was different. Each of us had to "teach" the class in a proof problem to be provided by the professor.

It was time. Mine had been provided a few days earlier and tomorrow was the day I had to perform. I had been so busy with all the rest of my schoolwork I gave little time to preparations, but I wasn't worried. I should have been. Late in the afternoon on the day before showtime I began to work the solution. I worked it and worked it, but to no avail. I was lost—and doomed for embarrassment and failure. It was near midnight. I decided to give it up and confront the professor with my defeat. I went to bed.

Suddenly, I woke up. "That's it," I said in a loud voice. I hopped out of bed, turned on the lights over my desk, and continued with my elation over my sleeping solution. "I got it, I got it," I kept saying.

Just then, Roger, my roommate, woke up from a deep sleep in his bunk across the room. "What the hell are you doing?" he groaned, after being startled awake by my overly exuberant zeal.

"Roger, I got it! I got it! I dreamed the answer. I don't know how I did it, I just did."

Looking at me like I had totally flipped, he just rolled over in his bunk. "Good, that's good," he whispered with a sigh. His breathing soon fell into a rhythm and I heard him snoring once again.

I finished my work and went back to bed feeling accomplished and saved. I woke up early the next morning thinking I had dreamt the whole thing. I sprang out of the sack and rushed over to the desk to see if it was for real or if it was a trick played by my very tired head. To my great relief and happy discovery, I found all my notes from last night. It was all in order. I left for class and presented my project. The class asked a few questions but they understood my solution. So did the professor.

I got my A. I felt so good. I remember thinking back to the time so long ago when I heard that mysterious woman tell me that my future was secure and not to worry. What she didn't tell me was the part about "There is no such thing as a free lunch." You have to work for what you get, and by God, I did that last semester and passed all my courses. Graduation came. I then had the distinct honor of being the first ever of my entire family to graduate college. I had a degree! And not just a degree, a double major in mathematics and chemistry. Now, I had to figure out what I wanted to do with it.

In addition to all of the hype with school I also had just gone through a very difficult time in my love life. I had for the first three years of college been seeing a wonderful girl named Janice. She was fifteen and I was seventeen when we first met. We were sure we were going to marry and so were our families. We made plans, talked about how many kids we were going to have, etc. We were too young to be that serious and eventually came to understand that. We grew apart. I had a few other dates while in school, but they were never serious until that one day in May.

It was late in May, just prior to graduation, when she came into my life. My wife-to-be. I knew her before, but never gave it any thought. I was visiting an old buddy one weekend and ended up on a double date, with me as a blind date for the sister of his girlfriend. It was a whirlwind romance but it stuck! She was perfect in every way. And, she was right there, where I grew up. In fact, her parents bought that old house of ours. Never did I think that when I took a girl home from a date it would really mean—**taking her home!**

This was an awakening in my life. So, in addition to getting my degree, I had fallen in love. She was a girl from that little place, that little town where I grew up. She was the girl of my dreams. The summer went by quickly and my focus was on the future. I had to work fast, time was short. I decided to enter the United States Air Force, having passed all the requisite tests—I was going to be a pilot. But first I had to go to commissioning school. The applications were filled out and submitted.

It was 20 July 1969. The Apollo program was in full swing at NASA and I with it, and on that historic day I asked my beloved to marry me. I told her before of my plans for the Air Force and that didn't scare her. She said yes. I was officially a committed man! Whew! I didn't think I would be able to take the ring back.

I arrived home and anxiously flung open the door to announce my engagement, and saw my dad sitting in front of that little black-and-white TV watching a blurry image from some old movie. I couldn't figure out why Dad, of all people, was so interested in an old movie on TV that he wouldn't take the time to listen to my most important piece of news. Hmm. Dad said it wasn't a movie, but a transmission to Earth from the Moon. In my love-struck sense of reality I had not been following what would turn out to be the second most important thing of all humanity—the first being my engagement, of course. We had landed on the Moon. Not knowing all of this, I announced to Dad that I was engaged. Mom was working so she was unable to take part in my celebratory glee.

"Shhh, sit down, they're landing on the Moon. Watch! Oh, by the way, you're stupid, but we'll cover that later," he said.

Well, not understanding a thing of what he was talking about, I obediently sat and watched. I was pissed! My announcement interrupted by this thing called the first lunar landing. So I waited. Eventually, I too was drawn in, taken by the enormous thing man had done. When the telecast ended, Dad got up and went over to the small library shelf and retrieved a book.

"What are you doing?" I asked.

"Did you give her any consideration?" he asked.

"Well, yes, I gave her a lot of consideration, I love her," I responded, wondering where all this was going. We had just landed on the moon and Dad was so engrossed, but now he wanted to know if I had given my bride-to-be any consideration. Did he think I was nuts?! Of course I considered her. A lot!

"No, I mean, did you give her something?" he said. All of a sudden I knew where he was going. He was a Teamsters' Union business agent and was taking a course in business law. He was acting the part of a lawyer.

Thinking he was serious, I responded, "Yes, I gave her a ring. Isn't that what you are supposed to do when you ask someone to marry you?"

"Well, yes, but I wanted you to understand that she has you cold. If you change your mind she has you for breach of contract."

"Huh?"

"Yeah, breach of contract. Either you follow through or she can sue you for a failed contractual promise," he said.

"Dad, come on. Give me a break. I just thought you would be happy for me."

"I am, son. I just want you to understand how serious this thing is. Now, what did you think of the Moon landing?"

"Well, Dad, to be honest, my mind was on bigger things lately. What do you think?"

"Gosh, the landing on the Moon was historic, wonderful, and great!" he said.

"No, damn it, my engagement."

"Oh, that. I just want you to know that it is no surprise to Mom or me, and of course it is fantastic. I was pulling your leg. Congratulations, son. More than two people landed on the Moon tonight," he said.

And that's the way it went. Celebrated the engagement and lunar landing the same day. Wedding was set for 27 December 1969. I was due to enter the Air Force Officer Training School on 3 October 1969, and after successful completion, enter pilot training at Craig Air Force Base in Selma, Alabama, on 4 January 1970. But before all that I had more to do…

FIVE

Now you have feathers
It's time to fly

It was midsummer 1969. The phone rang.

"Hey, good morning, this is your favorite recruiter."

"Good morning. What's up, Sergeant?"

"I mentioned before that you have to have a physical before we can go further. We set you up for a pre-induction physical in Chicago. It's at the Armed Forces Induction Center downtown. I have arranged all the necessary papers, tickets, and reservations for you. In fact, we will reimburse you for your meals. It's all set for early next week. Can you stop by later today to pick up the package?"

"Sure thing, thanks. I'll be there around one. One question, though; what can I expect to be put through down there?" I asked.

"Well, it's a full day. You will start off with a couple of simple tests and forms to fill out, and then they will guide you through the maze. You'll be given all the necessary immunizations so you won't have to do that when you get to San Antonio. Don't worry; it's nothing to fret about."

The rest of the week flew by and there I was, on a bus going to the Loop area of Chicago. I had never been there before. The ride was only about two hours but it felt like a million. That guy next to me stunk. Mostly booze, I think.

The sergeant had made a reservation for me at the YMCA downtown, which was centrally located and convenient to both the bus station and the Induction Center. Not the best part of town. I found the place, walked up to the desk and rang the bell. It was late afternoon. I was nervous. The clerk came out of the smoke-filled anteroom. A crusty gent, unshaven, and a bit heavy.

"What can I do for you, mister?" he asked, knowing by my appearance and the look on my face that I was slightly intimidated.

"I have a reservation," I said. I explained the reason for my stay and handed him a voucher ticket for the room.

"Here you go; it's on the twelfth floor, room 1214. Now let me explain the rules here, sonny. No noise after ten and no booze. The bathroom is at the end of the hall. You need to be considerate of others; some of them live here and believe it is theirs. Ain't no food in the building, just a couple of machines here in the lobby. There's a greasy spoon a block down on the other side of the street. Ain't much, but it's food. Put the key in this slot tomorrow when you leave."

Feeling quite alone and like I had just jumped into a scene from *The Twilight Zone*, I searched the lobby for the elevator, got in, and hit the twelve button.

The room, oh, that room. I opened the door and found the light switch on the right. One light—just a single bulb—dangling from a cord hung in the middle of the dingy little room. A window directly across from the door had no curtains, just a roll-up type of shade. I examined the view. Several stories down were the rail tracks of the elevated train that ran throughout the loop.

The single twin-size bed was pushed against the far wall, with a small stand next to it. There was no phone; it was in the hall, halfway down from my room to the toilet. A small black-and-white TV was at the foot of the bed against the wall. The room was clean, but that's about all. My dorm room in college was the Hilton in comparison.

I settled in as best I could. I wasn't hungry. I should have been, though. I knew tomorrow was going to be a long day, but that didn't matter. I turned the light off and lay back on my bed, thinking of all the possible things tomorrow would bring. Just then, I heard someone coughing. Sounded like it was in the room next door to mine—the walls were thin—I could even hear him fart. Yuck! I fell asleep but was startled awake by the train. It was all night long at intervals of about once an hour. *God, how in hell can anyone stay here?* I thought. One thing, though—the price was right!

The next day eventually came. The shower at the end of the hall was communal, too. No problem that morning, however—most of the inhabitants obviously didn't believe in taking them.

I readied myself and left for that greasy spoon the man had told me about. I had to be at the Induction Center by eight o'clock. I had an hour and half. I didn't need that long, so I took my time.

I found the center and walked up the steps. It was a huge building; nothing great, just a standard government-looking multistory structure. I opened the door and entered the main lobby. I found a sign giving directions for those like me who were there for physicals and testing. I followed the sign. Eventually

I found a large room and entered. There were already a lot of people there. Some official-looking person was handing out forms, so I approached him and started to ask for directions but was cut short.

"Just fill these out and sit down," he said rather tersely. I knew from the sound of his voice he didn't like his job. He apparently didn't like people, either. What a grouch! I found a pencil and started. The room continued to fill up with people.

I had just finished my forms when a man came in and introduced himself. He was a nicer man, simply dressed in an official-looking smock. He explained his position at the center.

"Okay, gents, give me your attention. You are here today to take the induction physical. Most of you will have no problem passing. You will receive any shots you need. You will each meet with a doctor. It is a fast pace and will take most of the day. If anyone here is not here for your pre-induction physical, you should leave now," he said.

No one left. He again stressed that the day would be long, but would be a lot shorter if we all did exactly what we were told. He mentioned that this center processed all persons for all services. It didn't matter that I was going to commissioning school in the fall. Some of these blokes were going almost immediately into the Army and basic training and from there likely to Vietnam.

There must have been at least two hundred of us. Most of us were in our late teens and early to mid twenties. We were dressed in just about every possible combination of garb. Some wore a suit and tie, others had holey jeans and tennis shoes, and I was in a casual shirt and slacks. We didn't talk much to each other. We knew that this was all a temporary thing and making friends was not something important—there wouldn't be time to develop any kind of relationship, anyway. We were nice to one another, however.

We entered the room. It was a large room. We were all issued a basket.

"Okay, gentlemen, I want all of you to strip down to your underwear, no T-shirts, put everything in the basket, and hold on to it until I tell you what to do with it. Leave your shoes on."

So there we were, all of us acting like little robots, getting naked down to our shorts. I suddenly realized that some of these men had not been near a washing machine in a long time. The room began to smell like the men's locker room in high school.

We handed over our baskets to another person, were given a receipt, and were told to sit down and wait for further instructions.

Next, we were divided into smaller groups. Some were going to get shots right away and others were going to see the doctors. It was like we were cattle. It occurred to me that we were going to trust these strangers to poke, prod, and shoot us up with crap, and all without objection.

"Okay. You, you, and down to you, follow me," he said. I was in this group. There must have been twenty of us. Strange, just one ahead of the other, in only our undershorts and shoes. Suddenly, we were face-to-face with people on either side of our line. They were armed with guns—air guns used to give immunizations. They obviously took great pride in their work and seemed to like the fact that they were going to inflict serious pain on our robotic bodies. One after another we took shots in both arms.

I was just two guys away from the men with the shot guns, when all of a sudden the man immediately in front of me fell to the floor and started to shake. I thought he was faking it. He was making strange sounds, his breathing was raspy, and he was drooling gobs of foamy crap from his mouth. Then, he started to pee his pants; pee was all over the place. His eyes rolled up in his head. He wasn't faking. God, this man is dying. What the hell was going on?

Almost immediately, a couple of official-looking men came to this guy's aid. They stuck something in his mouth and held him down until he calmed down. They helped him up and moved him out of the way.

Apparently, the man was an epileptic, and the fear of getting those shots put him over the edge. Needless to say, I had never experienced anything like that. After the man was removed from the line, we continued on.

Next stop—bend over. "Okay, gents, drop your shorts to your ankles, bend over, reach behind your ass and spread your cheeks." Suddenly the room went quiet, all of us looking at each other with disbelief. "I said, strip and bend over. NOW!" He wasn't kidding. Shyly we did what he said.

Boy! If the other room had smelled like a gym locker room, this room was even worse. Soon, a guy resembling a doctor and another man holding a clipboard strolled behind us, one by one. The doctor had a flashlight and some sort of throwaway probe. He muttered things to the other guy at his side as he went. Each of us was previously given a number. That's how he identified us to the other guy. I am not sure what the purpose of this portion of the exam was, but it was obvious to me that the doctor was not having fun. He wasted no time with each ass sticking and stinking in front of his face. As he passed behind us, he told us we could pull up our shorts. We wasted no time doing it. This was one of those times where, if I ever had any aspiration to be a doctor, I didn't anymore. The view from our angle was seriously ugly, but the view from the doctor's vantage point had to be worse.

It all **ended** up okay—no pun intended—and apparently I passed. The bus ride back was a relief. I wasn't sure whether what I had just witnessed was real or just a bad dream. Nevertheless, I was en route to friendly turf. A report would be filled out and mailed to my recruiter. The next time I would return would be when I was sworn in. That was to happen in the fall. I had a class start date of 3 October, and would be sworn in the morning prior to that.

That day arrived fast. My fiancée, my mom and dad, and I all drove down to Chicago. It was an exciting time for me—but again, scary. This time, though, I knew that I was not coming home, not for a few months. I was also sad because I was leaving behind the love of my life. It was going to be a long wait. We shook it off, though, trying to keep each other from tearing up. We arrived at the Induction Center. When we checked in, this time the people were different— nicer. No more cattle treatment. I thought they were doing that because I had witnesses with me.

We were all escorted to a nice room. There were many chairs, and at the front of the room were flags of all the services, with the U.S. flag in the middle. It was all over so fast. Once the oath of office was given, I and others who were heading for the Air Force were directed to follow one of the personnel for a short bus ride to O'Hare International Airport. I quickly gave my good-bye hugs and kisses, and with some tears I followed directions.

It was a two-hour flight to San Antonio. I tried to sleep but couldn't. It was a long way from that morning, when I was in the arms of my lovely woman. Now, I was alone with a bunch of scared young men. We were met at the airport by a sergeant in a Smokey Bear hat (also known as a campaign hat). He came right over to the gate and yelled, "All you people going to Lackland Air Force Base, stand over here next to the wall and keep quiet!" I suddenly realized that I had met my new mother. Only this time she was a he and ugly.

Next, after being given a few behavioral orders, we silently filed outside the terminal to a waiting Air Force bus. Next stop, the chow hall, and then the barracks.

We were still in our civilian clothes. Sweaty now, though. God, it was hot. The barracks were open bay. Must have been forty cots total, twenty on each side, with an open area in the middle. The toilets had no stalls. Each commode was totally open to the entire area. If you had to take a dump, you did it in front of everyone. Not much choice.

Next, that good-natured mother impostor again showed his face, and apparently he was not there to tuck us in. He must have thought we were all deaf because every time he said anything he yelled at us. We were all in a state of shock. He gave us the lights-out rules, and briefly explained that those of us in the room who were going to be officers would go to the Medina Annex (*wherever that was*) and the others would be redirected to another location. "Chow is at 0530 hours. You will have ten minutes to get your ass out of bed, showered, shaved, and standing in front of your bunk! Be ready!" he yelled.

I vowed that if I could get rid of this mother I would do everything I could to "be ready."

The next morning came with a scare of some idiot turning on every light in the place. I was startled awake and suddenly realized that the day before had not been a dream. I truly was in a different world. I quickly remembered we had only ten minutes to do the things that yesterday would have taken thirty. I did it, though. We were directed to a bus outside and off we went to the mess hall. Then, after a five-minute time allowance to scarf down breakfast, those of us designated for officer training were told to board a different bus. Next stop—OTS!

SIX

Not everything is assured
Trial before victory

Three months later—Craig Air Force Base…

I had graduated, was now a second lieutenant, married, and in pilot school—UPT (Undergraduate Pilot School). I was determined to be what my dad always wanted for himself and for me—a fighter pilot!

But first things first—we, the new class, had to meet the commander. Yup, just like the old days, a formal receiving line. The men were to wear their class A uniforms and the women HAD to have a veiled hat. I told my wife.

"What? They want me to wear what?" She looked shocked. I had no idea it would hit her that hard. There we were, married just a couple of weeks, and I was sure if she had a chance she would head for Wisconsin.

"Sorry, hon. That's what they said. Here, look at the flyer they gave us." I showed it to her.

"Where the hell am I going to find one of those, and what are we going to use for money?" she said.

"We'll have to do it. Somehow," I said. I knew we didn't even have enough money for pots and pans, and now we were being forced to spend more money we didn't have. This was at the time when credit cards were things of the future. But we did it. We found a hat and she got a cheap but nice-looking dress to wear.

Oh, she had to wear white gloves, too! We had faced the first hard test of our marriage, and we passed. So with that bit of formal crap behind us, on to flying...

Each flying day was pretty much the same as the last. It was a fifty-three-week training program. Half of the class would fly in the morning and the rest would be in the classroom. The next day would be the opposite. They drove us hard on the PT field, too. For the first few weeks we had to run the laps with lead weights on our ankles and back. Made us strong, but it nearly killed us.

Flight line formation was at 0530 hours. We usually stood five or six abreast and several rows deep. We had to undergo an open ranks inspection by one of the IPs (Instructor Pilots), then raised the flag and were dismissed to our respective instructors for a tabletop discussion of what we had covered yesterday and what we were going to do that day. If we had bad weather days, we had to make up these on the weekends. There were lots of rainy days in Alabama, even in January.

The first part of training was in the T-41—a six-week program using a Cessna 172. I did well. Then it was off to the jets: the T-37 for the next five months, and then hopefully the supersonic T-38. The T-37 was a twin-engine, subsonic, straight-winged, six-thousand-pound dog whistle, so named because of the terrible deafening shrill of the engines when in idle. I was excited. I was actually going to do something most people would give their firstborn to do—fly.

Flying the jet was not that difficult, but the pressures of the school were very demanding. They expected that, once shown how to do something in the air, the next day we would do it perfectly. Each day built on the previous one, accumulating a long list of flying skills you had to do perfectly each time. If you screwed up, you had a pink check mark on the list of tasks scheduled for training that day and you failed the ride. That would not be a good thing. We practiced in every possible manner: simulators, armchair flying, discussions, etc.

Even my wife helped. She would challenge me every night on my emergency procedures. The bold print had to be memorized. Every morning on the flight line we had an oral task given by one of the IPs. The IP would begin in front of the class of about thirty of us, placing us in an imaginary flight emergency. Once the setup was completed, the IP would call out a student to respond. "Sir, this is single-engine on take-off, I would…" And all the words spoken by the student had to be perfect, down to the letter. If not, the student would fail and have to be retrained prior to that day's flying.

The IPs generally were seasoned Vietnam returnees and somehow got stuck as instructors in UPT. Most didn't like their job and they often took it out on the students. They were great pilots and used to flying F-4s or some other high-performance plane. Now they were stuck in this overgrown dog whistle and they didn't like it. I don't think they had ever been to instructor charm school, either…

We were on takeoff and flying out of the pattern on our way to the auxiliary field, when all of a sudden I felt a hand grabbing my oxygen hose which was securely strapped to my face. The IP started to yank my head back and forth.

"What the hell are you doing, Lieutenant? Fly like I told you!" he yelled. "Do you see this? DO YOU SEE THIS?" Each time he said that, he would yank my head from one side to the other. "I told you to FLY CONTACT! You aren't looking outside at all! You ain't clearing the goddamned area!" he yelled. "Now fly this goddamn plane! Not clearing could kill you— do you understand me?" The yelling into the cockpit intercom eased. I was scared. This guy was serious.

"Yes, sir!" I yelled back into the mike. I had never been treated like that before, not even in OTS. *This guy is pissed, and what the hell is the rest of the ride going to be like?* I thought. I recovered and the rest of the ride went well. He didn't pink me out that day, but I learned a whole new appreciation for following the rules. Actually, on that ride I was doing pretty well on instruments. I had my vector and was on altitude. But it was not an instrument ride.

On another flight, all was going great and the IP and I were having a good conversation while on the way out to the area for some simple flying maneuvers, when all of a sudden the IP asked me in a rather quiet voice, "Are you going to hit that?"

I must have been focusing on my instruments again and not clearing. We had just gone through the ten–thousand-foot check. All was good. My oxygen lever was correctly configured. "Hit what?" I asked. Then I realized what he was talking about. We were not sup-posed to fly through clouds—yet. "Oh, no, sir," I said. The huge cumulus cloud was threatening and very close. Too big to fly around. Only one thing left to do: fly over it. I put the throttle to 100 percent and pulled the stick back. In a matter of a few seconds we were on top of it. I then recovered my original altitude and attitude. Throttle back and straight and level. In the process of recovery we were nearly weightless and my helmet felt like it was floating.

"Well, you didn't hit it. But we sure got a taste of some negative g's," he said. I could tell he thought I did well, but it probably wasn't what he would have done.

That's the way it went every day. I was learning a lot. Some days were better than others. Then all hell started to break loose. The party was over. Each day was more and more demanding. I was a mediocre student on the stick, but aced the classroom academics. Some of my fellow students were great and others were really struggling. I was somewhere in the middle. I put my thinking and attitude in afterburner, and decided that I had to get a lot more serious. But I wasn't having fun—until that one special day.

"Okay, let's bring this in and pull it over to the side," he said. We were flying the pattern. I thought I had done something wrong. Not this time. This time, everything was good. "Now, I want you to shut down the starboard engine and idle the port engine. Raise the canopy." I did what he said, wondering what he had in mind. He started to get out! "You are either going to fly this plane or you will die trying," he said. "Now, I'm getting the hell out and I give you the signal for engine start. Good luck, Lieutenant."

He did exactly what he said. He got out, stood back, and gave me the twirling finger to start the starboard engine. I lowered the canopy. I was alone in a jet for the very first time. I was slightly nervous, but remember saying out loud, "Okay, chump, it's now or never. You know what to do, so don't dick this thing up." I radioed the tower, "This is Tide 36, request instruction for takeoff."

"Tide 36, you are number one for takeoff." That was my cue to pull the plane on the runway, line it up, clear the area, throttle up, check engine instruments, and release the brakes. I had done this so many times dual that I didn't even think about the empty seat on my right. I was soloing. The plane felt good. I was flying! Me! Flying a jet! Although I was doing all the flying when dual, it meant more when I knew there was an empty seat on the right.

I was instructed to stay in the pattern and do as many touch-and-goes as I could with the fuel and time I had left. A typical flight was usually one and a half hours. I had about forty-five minutes left. I felt great. Takeoff, gear up, flaps up, attitude, climbing left turn to 1200 AGL(above ground level) to the out-side downwind corridor. Then a left turn to the inside leg, halfway down the strip which was immediately be-low me, perform a sixty-degree left-bank pitchout ma-neuver, maintain altitude, throttle back, speed break out. Flaps, gear down at 150 KIAS (Knots Indicated Airspeed). Maintain altitude; check the ground, line up for final turn. Slow to 110 KIAS. Start the descend-ing turn, line up and aim at the strip overrun. Flare at 100 KIAS. Touch down. Same routine, over and over.

"Okay, Tide 36, bring it down full stop. That was a good first day solo." Those magic words became indel-ibly imprinted in my memory.

I landed as instructed and parked the plane on its spot on the tarmac. I secured the plane and performed my logging. What happened next was about the next best thing to soloing. As I approached operations, sev-eral classmates suddenly came out of the building with a pail of water. I got doused. It was customary to be so indoctrinated after your first solo. It felt so good. I made it! Well, I thought I did. On the way home that day I made a stop at the O Club for some well-deserved celebratory beer. What was also customary was to buy your IP his choice booze, usually a fifth of whatever he wanted. I did that, too. I couldn't wait to tell my bride and call my dad.

I thought I had the tiger by the tail for quite a while after my first solo. Things were about to change. I don't know why, but somehow I was not flying consistently. I was starting to fail rides. Each day's ride demanded more than the last and therefore became more difficult. I felt like a flunky. My good attitude was under attack. I began getting depressed, but didn't say anything to my wife. Not right away. I was failing pilot school, or at least it felt that way. To make matters worse, my mom and dad made a special trip, driving from Wisconsin to Selma, Alabama, to share in my accomplishments. It was only two weeks since that first solo. I had a few other solo flights which were good, but every time I went dual I would screw up something and pink the ride. I didn't mention any of this to Dad. His pride was so deep. I didn't have the heart to tell him his fighter-pilot-to-be son was not making it, but I wasn't giving up. At least I thought I was giving it everything I could. Once you're behind the power curve it gets harder and harder to recover. It was a steep hill to climb.

Then something even scarier began. I came home to our little trailer house after one very trying day on the flight line. I opened the door and found my brand-new wife looking pale and quite sick. She said she had been vomiting a lot lately, usually in the morning. She couldn't keep anything down. I checked her over as best I could, but found nothing. She wasn't feverish.

"Feel this," she said, placing my hand on her lower abdomen.

"I can't feel anything," I said.

"No, here!" She took my hand again, and this time I felt a hard spot. *Oh my God, what the hell is that?* I thought. I was scared.

"How long has this been going on?" I asked.

"Well, on and off for a few weeks," she said. "I think it's getting worse. I didn't want to worry you so I didn't tell you. Besides, you have a lot on your mind with your training."

Pilot school was not going well, and now I had quite probably a very sick woman. I immediately told her to get her purse because we were going to the flight surgeon on the base.

We waited outside the doctor's office and finally my wife was admitted in. It was an unscheduled appointment—we got lucky.

I sat there, waiting. It felt like an eternity. I was worried. She had a lump down there and was sick mostly in the morning. I knew she had had some anemia when she was young, but this was not that kind of thing. This was serious. At last the door opened. I looked for my wife to come out, but she remained inside.

"Lieutenant. Please come in and have a chair," he said. He was a captain, but a doctor, too.

"Yes, sir," I replied. "Sir, is it serious?"

"Lieutenant, I don't want to worry you, but yes, it is serious. Very serious. We'll have to do some tests to be sure what we've got here, but believe me, it is serious."

I was almost shaking. "Do we need to go to the regional hospital in Montgomery?"

"No, I don't think that would help in this situation."

"Is it cancer or something?"

"Lieutenant, I have to tell you that what's wrong with your wife is most likely your fault."

"My fault? How could that be?" I was getting really confused.

"You dumb shit, your wife is pregnant," he replied. "And I believe you are the one that impregnated her, right?"

I was immediately propelled into orbit. My wife was pregnant! God, the morning sickness, and all that. Yes, I was a dumb shit—but a happy one. I was going to be a dad. I had to be careful with her. The doctor laughed and so did my wife. I had been duped, but somehow it didn't matter. He gave us some direction and set up an appointment with anther doctor that was an obstetrician. We left the doctor's office. I was so concerned I held on to her as we walked to the car. I even opened the door for her, something I hadn't done for quite a while.

So, even though my piloting was not going well I felt some glee. We were going to be parents. It didn't take long before the reality of the event we had just experienced set in. The responsibility of it all! Wow! We called our folks and spread the word.

The newness of pregnancy soon wore off. I had to keep my mind on my training. It was tough, though. I continued my struggles at school. Some days were better than others. If you pink a ride you have to fly it again, and you have only three chances to get it right. I did this and was barely keeping up with the class. For some reason, even the positive influence of my solo flights on my flying had waned. I was in trouble. I finally broke the news to my wife.

"What are we going to do, hon?" she asked. "If you fail, where will they assign you?"

"I don't know, but I'm a little scared about what the future is going to bring. Our first consideration is for the baby. Don't worry, something will break. I just don't know what, or when," I responded.

Things continued to deteriorate in school. Eventually, I had flown all the possible rides to do what I could to recover and get back on track. I had never in my life failed anything, but I was failing UPT. What would I tell Dad? Where would we go? I failed the eighty-eight and ninety-nine rides. Those were the check rides with an IP whose job was to see if there was any hope for the student. Next step was a faculty board.

I met the board. It was a panel of IPs—none of them mine. It felt like a court martial. It didn't take long—about two hours. The board heard my case and soon made the decision. I was to be removed from flight status and placed on casual status until I was given orders for the next assignment. The pressure was off, but I felt like a first-class loser. My wife married a loser. I became very depressed. I prayed a lot. Yes, I even thought about that place long ago—that place where those women visited me when I was so young. I guess I proved them wrong. My future was not so secure after all. I was ashamed and down.

I had to pull myself together. I had a loving wife and a child on the way. I made a vow to myself that I would never fail anything again! I meant it, too. I would excel at whatever assignment I got next. *I learned later that over 50 percent of my class was eliminated and that the needs of the Vietnam War were not as high as they had been in prior months.*

My assignment finally came. I was headed for Sheppard Air Force Base at Wichita Falls, Texas. I was going to be a Titan II Missile Launch Officer. I was going to be trained to launch nuclear weaponry on our enemies—primarily, the Soviet Union. Training was a fourteen-week course at Sheppard, then off to Vandenberg Air Force Base in California for a bit more training, and then to McConnell Air Force Base near Wichita, Kansas, for launch officer crew duty. It was amazing—from airplanes to rockets…

I was just twelve when I heard about a rocket launched at someplace called Vandenberg. I needed to go there someday, I told Dad. He would smile and give me an encouraging look, as if he knew something I didn't.

Yes, I had my shot at being a fighter pilot and blew it. But I realized that desire was the key to success. Maybe I didn't want it badly enough. I'll never know. I wanted to make Dad proud; he never achieved that goal to the level he really wanted. He wanted the best for me and I knew it.

Dad was my inspiration in those early years. Sometimes, he would get me out of bed in the wee hours of night to show me stuff in the sky—comets, falling stars, etc. He and I would always talk about the mysteries of the night and what might exist way out there in the sky.

I was definitely into rockets. As a kid I built them, launched them, and read every book I could that had anything to do with them or space in general. Space and everything connected to it was always my dream. Honestly, I never felt that much passion for airplanes, though I loved flying. But I wanted to be a part of space in any way I could.

My life after pilot school changed a lot. I now found myself in the field I loved when I was so young— rockets. I didn't care if they were a war machine, I loved them.

I became content to do whatever the Air Force told me to do, as long as I could wear the uniform I so much loved. The Air Force decided I was better suited to be a missile launch officer for the Titan II and Minutemen ICBMs (Intercontinental Balistic Missiles), and I agreed. With the gnawing pain of having failed pilot school, I promised myself I would never fail again. I didn't; in fact, I excelled.

Yes, I made it to that place far away, a place called Vandenberg Air Force Base, at first for training and then as a permanent assignment. I had my assignments at McConnell for Titan II, and then at Ellsworth AFB for Minuteman missile crew duty, then eventually ended up at Vandenberg as a member of the faculty of the Strategic Air Command (SAC) 4315th Combat Crew Training Squadron.

SEVEN

Space
To explore
To learn
To realize your dream

The phone rang, startling me—I had just nodded off. I reached over to answer. Who could this be? There I was in the motel at the Cape, having just returned from the O&C (Operations and Checkout) building and the crew after what seemed like two days of work jammed into one, and had finally settled into the sack. I looked at the clock. It was just a little after six p.m. I had just finished a snack from the vending machine and retired, feeling exhausted. I must have been asleep for about two hours, though.

"Hello," I answered in a groggy voice, wondering who it could possibly be. Hopefully, my family back in Houston was okay. My wife and sons were alone a lot lately. I was sure the boys wondered where Daddy went so often. My wife is a strong woman and has always been there for me and our boys. I love them so.

"Hey, sorry about the short notice. This is Crip. Did I wake you?" he said, knowing he had. "I need to change the schedule a little for later today. A little overtime for ya," he quipped. "Get a couple hours of shut-eye and come in around ten tonight. I want to cover any procedural changes that might be required from the OMI documents. We don't have a lot of time so I want to get it done as soon as possible. I already snagged Larry before he left for the day. He'll be here, too. It shouldn't take maybe about three hours or so, okay?"

"No problem, sir," I replied, knowing there was no other answer.

"Thanks, bud, see you in a couple. The coffee will be on."

I am here to work the mission and that is what I will do, no matter what it takes, I thought. At least I didn't have to contact Larry Dunn, my lead in the FDF world. FDF is short for Flight Data File, or flight procedures. It was not the usual thing to have the astronauts calling direct, but when working the mission we all worked together. Bob Crippen was a fantastic guy. This would be his first mission into space and the fifth for John Young, including two lunar missions. I was proud to be a part of the support team.

I was assigned to the crew as direct support in the area of crew procedures development. My job was to ensure the crew was happy with anything and everything about their flight documents, which amounted to approximately sixty-five pounds of documentation. All this for the first Space Shuttle mission. I didn't go to the Cape every time the crew went, but whenever there were major tests in readiness for the mission someone had to be there that could work the details of crew procedural deltas.

The technical impacts to these documents could come from many sources, but the crew had to be happy with all of them. We were preparing for the world debut of the Space Transportation System. Columbia was her name and she waited on Pad 39A. Our country's first Space Shuttle, and Bob Crippen (pilot) and

John Young (commander) were its crew. Launch date was set for 10 April 1981, with a seven a.m. liftoff, and we had lots to do before that date. It was many years in the planning, starting long before I was chosen from many to be a part of it. I reflected back to the beginning...

It was early spring 1980.

Like a conscientious young officer, and being near the end of my tour at Vandenberg, I began working my contacts for a follow-on assignment, which I believed would be still in SAC. I had just finished a full day in the classroom and returned to my desk to prepare for tomorrow's lesson when my desk phone rang. My destiny was about to change.

"Hello," I answered, and introduced myself. The man's voice on the other end was strange to me, but he spoke with a certain authority.

"Just who I am looking for. This is Colonel Rinebold from MPC." He explained his role at MPC (Military Personnel Center) in officer assignments. "I know you are aware that your current tour there at Vandenberg is coming to an end, and I'm sure you're working your network for your next assignment, but I have the opportunity of a lifetime just pounding on your door, Captain." He went on, "We are looking for smart, highly technical people to fill a one-of-a-kind billet. We think you are the right guy for the job."

"What is that, sir?" I replied hesitantly. This colonel was a total stranger to me and he came across like a used car salesman. I wasn't sure where all this was going, but one doesn't usually get a personal call from MPC directly. I listened.

"We want you to go to Texas—specifically, Houston, Texas. We want you to be part of a select group of officers to work various jobs, as NASA decides, in support of the Space Shuttle program." He went on to describe the process of selection. An Air Force central selection board had already met and I was one of hundreds throughout the Air Force to have been screened and won the final selection.

This was all news to me. I had no idea that was going on. It was to be a joint selection process. First, the Air Force did theirs, and then they were to submit the short list to NASA—Johnson Space Center. NASA had to agree or it was off. Because the duty was voluntary, the colonel wanted my approval to forward my package to NASA at the Johnson Space Center. I felt high honor that all this was going on and that I was hand-picked from hundreds of officers. I didn't even know what I was getting into or perhaps agreeing to, but it was "space stuff" and it was NASA. It had to be good!

"Needless to say, sir, I am stunned and excited at the same time. How much time do I have?" I asked. "I would like to discuss it with my wife. By the way, you must be aware that I know nothing about manned spaceflight. I launch bombs on rockets and teach others to do the same."

"I understand. I know all about your experience, Captain, don't worry. Twenty-four hours," was his answer. "Sorry about the short notice, but we are all working on a rather complicated arrangement with NASA. They are asking for our input soon. I might add that NASA isn't totally in favor of this whole thing, but they decided to work with us but we don't want to piss them off." He went on, "Your efforts in Houston will be in preparation for a like program currently in the making for the Air Force. The Air Force is going to have its own shuttle program—a blue shuttle. The

Air Force is vastly changing the way we place satellites in space—direction from the highest level. We need people to operate this program and they need to be trained. You are one of those people," he said. "You have an impressive record and the right education, and we think NASA will like what they see in you."

"Wow! Thank you, sir. I'll contact you tomorrow," I responded. He gave me his contact number at MPC at Randolph AFB in San Antonio, Texas.

I was so excited about this I wasn't sure what to do. I couldn't wait to get home and talk it over with my wife, and let our two sons in on the deal. Even my local bosses were unaware of the program just revealed to me by the colonel.

I came back the next day with an agreement to go ahead with the NASA selection input. When the colonel answered the phone, he laughed a bit and thanked me, but added, "Captain, now I am going to make your life even more complicated. After we talked yesterday, your name also came up for an assignment to the Naval Postgraduate School up in your neck of the woods at Monterey, California."

I was stunned. "What would I be doing there?" I asked.

"Something called 'C-cubed-I.' I think it stands for Communications, Command, Control, and Intelligence," he said. "You will be given an assignment there to earn a master's degree in that area. Sounds like a good opportunity for you, too. It's a job heavy in mathematics and you have the credentials. You're a pretty lucky guy. Most people don't get these opportunities."

"Yes, sir. Thank you, sir. But what about the NASA thing?" I asked, my head spinning.

"Well, depending on what you tell us, we will pursue the corresponding path," he said. All of a sudden, I was propelled into a whole different Air Force. They do not typically give a crap what you want to do—they tell you what they want and then you do it. He gave me some more details of the Monterey thing, then left it for me to decide.

"When do you need my response, sir?" I asked.

Laughing again, he said, "Tomorrow." Apparently, the Air Force Institute of Technology (AFIT), a university system within the Air Force, had developed this new program to fill a growing demand in the area of intelligence and needed officers trained appropriately for those follow-on assignments.

"Okay, thank you, sir. I want to discuss this with my wife, too," I said. I put the phone down.

Now I was propelled into a high state of confusion. What to do! My head was swirling. All this was happening so fast. Why me? I already had a master's degree and really didn't want or need another. The idea of working in the manned space program was a dream come true, even though I had zero experience in it. But, what to do! Typically, my wife said it was up to me. She would support me no matter which direction we chose. What a gal. We were both honored by all the attention and high praise from headquarters personnel, but I never thought about ever being considered for such things. I was just another Air Force ground-pounding dog that wanted to wear the uniform, which I did with tremendous pride. Okay, so I decided. NASA! With that behind me, I notified the colonel the next day as promised.

It was a few weeks later that I was officially notified of my selection. I was one of thirteen officers (all of us captains nearing promotion consideration to major—this assignment would surely help) to be assigned to the Johnson Space Center at Houston, Texas. It was 1980 and the world premiere flight of the shuttle was nearly a year away. I was nervous but excited. My life was to make a clear change. The impact of this change would permanently alter my life and those of my family, but it would be good. So now, on to Houston.

I had to find a place to live in Houston, hopefully near the space center. I had a home in California to sell or rent. We had no money, except the equity in the house. My Vandenberg bosses authorized a permissive trip to Houston for house-hunting, but this was to be on my nickel. I had to do this by myself, leaving my family in California while I sought out a home. It was only a five-day trip.

There was no active Air Force base there and therefore government housing was nonexistent. Ellington Air Force Base was located just north of the space center, but it was not an active base—one left over from the World War II days. NASA used a portion of it to support its flight operations. We had to live like everyone else—off the economy, without a lot of pampering from the Air Force. I landed at the main airport at dusk and in the middle of one of the worst rainstorms I had ever experienced. I remember thinking, *why would anyone want to come here?* It was hot, muggy, rainy, and flat. Ultimately, however, I made my way down the I-45 freeway to the NASA 1 exit in Clear Lake City. I found my way to the motel I had reserved, thinking how anxious I was to see what the area looked like in the daylight.

Morning came, the sun was shining and things looked a lot better. I had breakfast and hopped into the rental car and took a short tour of the area. I found the Space Center. Wow! It looked like a college campus. I was to meet a military sponsor there. His name was Lieutenant Colonel Gill Bonse. His office was in Building 1. They numbered all the buildings there. This was the tallest, with nine floors, and where most of the center's bigwig's offices were located. Gill's office was on the sixth floor.

Gill extended his hand. A short and slightly pudgy guy with a smile. Nice guy, perhaps too nice to be a lieutenant colonel, I remember thinking. "Hello, Captain, I'm Gill," he said. "Welcome to Houston. We are really glad you are going to be part of the team." After a few moments of introductions in his office area he took me around the center for a short tour, knowing my main purpose was to find a home for my family.

The air was thick and sticky and extremely warm, and had the odor of the nearby chemical plants. Ah— beautiful Houston! Although the center was beautifully laid out, I learned later that it was placed in the middle of a large filled-in swamp. They must have got a good price. It was only a few feet above sea level.

The contacts I had made before this trip allowed me to be quickly successful in finding a home. A new one in Webster, Texas, near Clear Lake City! It had four bedrooms and 1,800 square feet, compared to the small three-bedroom home of 1,300 in California. I never thought I could buy anything that expensive with no money and only a promise to buy, if and only if I could sell my home in California. Well, I did! I must add that one should never buy a home for the family without the missus. I made my share of mistakes. She was understanding, but would sometimes remind me of some of my deficient thinking while purchasing. The kitchen was dinky. That was my biggest sin. It was a sprint to the end, but the relocation happened.

I was assigned to the Flight Operations Directorate (FOD), Crew Procedures and Development Branch, in Building 4—a three-story building. The astronauts were located on the top floor. Mine was on the second.

Our new NASA bosses were numerous. The place I was assigned was in the FOD under the leadership of Mr. George Abbey. He had quite a distinguished history with NASA in the early years, but also had quite an attitude. I should point out that George was not happy having uniformed personnel at JSC (Johnson Space Center).

*A rule levied on the Air Force by George Abbey was that anyone working close to the crew would not wear a service uniform. It was barely acceptable to do so at our Houston offices throughout the Center, but never while working with the crew where there was a chance of high visibility. He fought our presence at the Center, but ceded to the Air Force. A most uncomfortable atmosphere for people like me. Apparently, George didn't have the most affection for the Air Force. These were **his** astronauts and his turf. A very difficult man to understand and the astronauts knew he had their flight future in his hands. The Air Force trainees like me came to learn this.*

Mr. Gene Kranz, George's deputy in FOD, held no such views. His focus was and remained the mission. He also was a key supporter to us. He knew others needed to learn, too. I learned later that, among many other firsts in manned spaceflight pathfinding for our country's space program from its inception, it was Gene who led the team as flight director for the cursed Apollo 13 mission back in April 1970. Later, there would be a movie by actor and motion picture director Ron Howard telling the story of this historic mission. Gene Kranz was a truly wonderful, but very direct man. No pussyfooting around! I liked that quality in people.

Indeed, I was surrounded by space heroes. There I was, about to be thrust into the mix and rubbing shoulders with the physical and mental elite—and in many cases world-famous people. I was classified a trainee and directed to work for NASA in positions they would decide.

"You'll be working in the Crew Procedures Development Branch. Your job will be to learn the shuttle systems, create procedures, and be involved with training the astronauts," said Gill. "We turn ourselves over to them and do what they tell us. We are guests here, so we have little to say about anything. Oh, one more thing; periodically, you will be asked to brief Gene on the progress you are making. I will let you know when that will happen. Right now your job is to get settled, get your family comfortable. You will report to Mr. Dan Bland as soon as you can. In fact, let's see if we can find him now to introduce you to him. He should be in the corner office here."

Once in Bland's office, Gill said, "Hello, Mr. Bland, here is your first trainee." Gill introduced me and explained my arrival schedule.

"Hi. I think we should sit down and have a little get-acquainted session whenever you are settled and are ready to go to work," Bland said. "Oh, technically you are a trainee, but as far as NASA is concerned you are one of the team, and therefore one of us.

We all have things to learn, so don't feel like you're the guinea pig."

"Where will I be working?" I asked.

"Ed and I believe you will fit well in the FDF world. Ed is my boss, Ed Pavalka. He runs this branch and I am a section lead under him, and lead the development of the crew procedures, among other things."

"May I ask what FDF is?" I asked, feeling a bit overwhelmed.

"Flight Data File, or crew procedures. From what I have been told, and understanding your history in the Air Force, you will be perfect for the job. Once you get settled I will introduce you around and let you get a feel for the area. By the way, we all work for the crew in the FDF world. We'll talk more later when you are finally settled. Welcome aboard. By the way, you can call me Dan."

I was getting the distinct feeling of being in a swimming pool and just learning how to swim, and I didn't have a clue where the life preserver was.

I finally found my way around. One important stop was the library, where all of the pertinent shuttle systems manuals were stored, as well as a rather large dictionary of NASA acronyms. NASA can't do anything without speaking in letters, which all contain volumes of meaning. I was in an office with three others. I was the only blue-suiter. The others were contractors. We all had jobs in the procedural world. So there I was—no definition to my trainee work. NASA apparently believed the best way to learn was to jump in. My first assignment was to assist a guy named John Bearly in the Orbit Pocket checklist—a sort of emergency procedural book covering most any potential on-orbit anomaly. Once in a while, one or two of the astronauts would drop in to discuss a matter of the technical content. Sally Ride came by often. She was new to the astronaut world, and later would gain world fame as our first female astronaut. Judy Resnik also would drop by for similar reasons. Judy would later die in the Challenger catastrophe. What a terrible loss. Bob Crippen would sneak in, too, sometimes to talk to Bearly on some technical issue of the Orbit Pocket checklist. What a great guy. Very down-to-earth. Little did I know that he and I would be working so closely.

My alarm scared the crap out of me. I was sound asleep. Suddenly, remembering what Crip had said, I knew I had to get myself together and get back to the space center. I quickly dressed and threw myself behind the wheel of the car. It was just a ten-minute drive from the Polaris Motel just behind the famed Apollo-era Mouse Trap nightclub to the crew quarters in the Operations and Checkout (O&C) building. This was where all the astronauts stayed. It had a suite of several bedrooms, a full kitchen, lounge, briefing room, and a small gym with a Jacuzzi. In all, quite comfortable. Crip was to meet me and Larry in one of the offices within that suite. I was entering the building and saw Larry coming from down the hall and entering the elevator. He waved.

I stopped by our FDF office on the second floor to check for messages from Houston, should there be any that would impact our evening's work. There weren't any. I scampered down to the elevator and hurried to the third floor to meet with Crippen.

"Hey, thanks for coming, guys. I really appreciate it. With the big test coming up I wanted to be sure we had all we needed in the Ascent Checklist and cue cards. I was looking through some of the late changes to the OMIs and it occurred to me we need to check them against the flight procedures. Hey, let's get going. The coffee's hot, help yourselves," he said. There weren't too many folks hanging around that late in the day. Crip had the reputation of being a workaholic and was proving it to us that night! We dove into the OMIs and the procedures. After a time we all took a breather. Larry left to check something in bonded stows, so it was just Crip and I sort of kicking back a bit, with our feet up on the edge of one of the desks.

"So, Crip, I have to ask you a question. Do you mind?"

"No, not at all—shoot."

"Well, my background is in ICBMs and I have some experience with solid rocket boosters," I said. "What I am wondering is what level of confidence you have with the SRBs, knowing they have only been ground fired tested and never yet flown."

"Ah, I see your concern. But, hell, the SRBs are the safest system of the entire vehicle," he said, cracking a slight smile.

"So, you're not concerned?"

"Oh, I didn't say that. The vehicle is extremely complicated, and what we are doing is a first for many areas. I think the TPS is likely to give John and me the most challenge," he said.

He knew I was aware of the TPS, or Thermal Protection System, and its complications, but I wanted more, so I just absorbed whatever Crip would discuss.

"What do you mean?" I asked.

"Well, those tiles cover the entire vehicle and we cannot afford to lose any, especially in certain critical areas. They are glued on and we hope they stay on. They are light and very brittle. This is a first—and it's extremely new technology. The forces acting on the vehicle during all phases of flight are extreme and anything could go wrong to disturb those tiles. That is the biggest concern I have. What we have to do is anticipate all possible anomalies and know how to respond to them. We are doing that. You're helping with that, in the procedures development area. Training is critical! I think we are ready. But I appreciate your concern. Any more questions?"

"No, sir, not yet. I really appreciate your candor, though. I must also say that I regard working with you and John and the rest of the team as an honor and a privilege. I am learning a lot. Thanks for being patient." After I said that, I thought he might think I was just sucking up. I hoped not, because I didn't do that crap.

Regarding those tiles, I knew there was no way we could help them if they lost any. Some of them are "okay" to lose, but the ones in key areas (wings, nose, and underbelly) would be terminal for the crew. Indeed, this was the biggest threat! NASA had no plan for handling this failure then and still doesn't today.

"Hell, you are doing great, and I am happy you're part of it," he said. "Coffee?"

We finished up earlier than anticipated. I left for the motel to get some badly needed rest. Tomorrow was another full day, then back to Houston. We had lots to do at the center to ensure we had everything right. The CDDT, or Dry Countdown Demonstration Test, scheduled for 19 March was fast approaching. The importance of this test was to exercise the countdown and count up activities with the crew and orbiter in otherwise full launch configuration. It is called "dry" because the vehicle had no propellants on board during this test, but many of the shuttle systems and the entire flight control team would be exercised.

My NASA bosses must have trusted me to allow me, a plebe, to be working so close to the crew. They encouraged me like big brothers, and for that I will always be grateful. Dan Bland, another workaholic, was extremely busy, so having a person he could trust to more or less take his place was a big help. Ordinarily, he would have to go on these short visits to the Cape. He took a few trips with me prior to this time to acquaint me with the area and how the Kennedy Space Center operated, but later left things pretty much up to Larry and me. That was a huge statement of trust!

The calendar flew by; there were lots of simulations in Mission Control for the team. I was assigned to the Ascent Team or "Silver Team" in the Flight Activities Officer's Staff Support Room (FAO SSR) just off the main control room. Each major player in the main room had an SSR to assist. In ours, we had several positions, in addition to mine for FDF. The main responsibility was to assist the front room, or MOCR (Mission Operations Control Room), with sound technical support for all crew activities, spacecraft attitude, and crew procedures updates.

After a few days, it was time to return to Florida and to the Cape to support the CDDT. The routine was pretty much the same: land commercially in Orlando, find a rental car, and drive for about an hour straight east to Cocoa Beach. This time was no different. I had no time to first check into the motel. I needed to get some crucial documents required for the test to bonded stows.

It was mid afternoon, the sun was high above, and that made the drive from Orlando easy, considering that my usual arrival time was late and after dark. Fog and animals crossing the Bee Line toll road were always a threat—either that, or the mating love bugs that smashed against the window during the spring mating time, in which case the cheap rental never had enough window cleaner.

I had just passed the Causeway Bridge, which spans the Banana River and connects Cape Canaveral to the Kennedy Space Center, and approached the O&C building when I heard a very close-sounding helicopter. Although there are lots of flying aircraft of different types in the area on either the NASA or the Air Force side of the river, this one sounded unusual. I slowed my vehicle to see if I could spot it, but by the time I pulled over the thing had gone from view. I remember it sounded very different.

"Oh, well," I said out loud. "I'd better get these documents to stows." My destination was just a couple of miles ahead on the left, a huge three-story building NASA called the O&C, or Operations and Checkout Facility. It had many functions. There was a high bay where specialized experiments were horizontally processed for future flights on the shuttle, seemingly hundreds of offices, and most importantly for me, the astronaut crew quarters located in a sectioned-off area of the third floor.

This trip was not going to be like the others. Although we were still a month or so away from our planned launch date of 10 April, I was unaware that we were in for a huge surprise.

I parked my car in my usual spot and grabbed the secure briefcase containing some cue cards and other assorted items which needed protection in bonded stows. It was a short walk to the rear door entrance. I got the thick pile of badges and sorted out which ones I would require. NASA had a badge for everything, but if you were to get near the crew you likely had the most.

I entered the elevator and punched number three. Only a short ride to the top floor, but the elevator was easier. The door opened. To the left and down the short hall was the guard station, in front of the double access doors to the first area or office area of the crew quarters. Around the corner and down about three doors on the left was bonded stows. When the crew was on station, the guards were seemingly more serious about their duty. I knew most of them since I had been there so many times before.

The guard station was a makeshift location, a table with a lone guard sitting behind it in a folding chair. It was located just a few feet away from the double doors to the crew quarters. The guard was a familiar face. Short, a bit chunky around the middle, with white hair and a small mustache, thinly trimmed. A pair of glasses shoved to the tip of his nose which aided in reading. He looked up, eyes focusing on me above the glasses. Yes, he was a familiar face, but I couldn't remember his name.

"Hello, young fella," the guard said, acknowledging my approach. "I suppose you are here for the festivities."

"Sure am," I replied. "Lots more security than normal," I added.

"Well, we have a special visitor here today. Here, let me check your badge." He checked them like he had never seen them before.

"Who?"

"Not allowed to say right yet," he said.

"I won't be here long, got to put this stuff into stows," I said.

I was cleared to proceed down the hallway, wondering if the sound I had heard outside was connected with the special visitor now contained in the crew quarters suite. Both Bob Crippen and John Young were there. The parking lot seemed full this time, but I thought, *well, this is a big test and we have a lot of people to work it.* So it all made sense. I went down the hall and found the door to bonded stows. A man just inside the door greeted me.

"I have some items for you," I said. He nodded, examined my package, and placed it on a shelf behind him, then handed me the log. I logged in the items and was about to leave when I heard a voice from down the hall calling my name. It was the lead support crew astronaut, Loren Shriver.

"Hello, Loren, how's it going? I just placed these items in stows. They are all yours now."

"Thanks, I'll get to them a bit later." He smiled and acknowledged what I had done.

Just then, the crew quarters doors opened and out came a bunch of guys wearing running duds, followed by John and Crip and the special guest (also in running shorts). It was none other than George H. W. Bush, the vice president of the United States. Wow! I hadn't been given even a clue that we would be getting this kind of attention, especially for a test and not the real thing. He looked around and shook a few hands (mine included), and then went with the crew to the elevator for a run. *He's a bit skinny,* I remember thinking, *and those shorts are certainly borrowed.* Must have had a few extras inside—skinny legs!

Apparently, this visit was planned well ahead of time and President Reagan was supposed to visit, but he had been hospitalized after the assassination attempt and was not able to travel. He sent the veep.

So they went running, and the tempo of the place settled down a bit once the crew and the vice president were out of the facility. I couldn't imagine they would be gone too long. Whew! What a day that turned out to be. I was close to a couple of presidents before in my life (Eisenhower and Ford), and now I could add Bush to the list, even though he was just a veep. With all that was happening to me in those days, being blessed to rub shoulders with the leaders of the nation's space program, and now the attention being placed on this somewhat obscure location by world-class leaders, I was truly in awe. As a boy, I remembered the Mercury, Gemini, and Apollo programs, and this place was where all the action emanated from. Now I was in the thick of a new era of space, a new investment in our country maintaining leadership in space exploration, and I had somehow become a part of it.

I was about to leave the facility for my hotel when Loren asked me to come in the suite for a beer. Surprised, I accepted. The crew was still out doing their thing, but inside the suite was a crowd that must have been there for some time before I arrived in the area. I must have been there about thirty minutes or so. Seemed longer, though.

So inside I went, finding myself in the midst of some very important people. In the lounge was a large round table, where I found astronauts Engle and Truly—the backup crew and the ones selected to fly STS-2. There were numerous others of the support team: Loren, of course, Larry Dunn, and many more. It was a buzz of activity. Oh, George Abbey was there, too, of course. Off to the left were senior NASA officials from Washington, Dr. Lovelace, and Mr. James Beggs. Lovelace was acting director, but Beggs would eventually take the job, although not until after the first mission. I again found myself thinking, *what the hell am I doing here?* I didn't object and soaked it all in. I was being introduced to so many folks I could not keep them straight.

Suddenly, the crew and vice president returned and disappeared in the back—I would assume to freshen up. I was in awe of the moment and didn't say much. I didn't want to say something stupid. I employed something Dad taught me many years ago: "You can usually fool everyone around you into believing you are much smarter than they are if you stay quiet and look intense, but once you open your mouth, you will immediately tell them exactly how smart you are. Most of the time it will demonstrate the not-so-smart side."

Suddenly, it became obvious it was time to leave the suite and be on my way. Tomorrow was to be a hugely busy day, starting very early for Larry and me. Part of my duties was to set up a briefing with the crew with Houston on closed-circuit TV, to cover launch weather and to update the Ascent Checklist for the weather parameters. The crew would use this to update the GPCs—General Purpose Computers—that would enable the orbiter to fly through the atmosphere on the way uphill. In order to do that, I had to get there early. I should mention another of my additional duties. It was during this time of the mission preparations that I was to program two Hewlett Packard calculators with an already prepared tape. The purpose of these handheld devices was to provide added assurance in flight for the calculations for CG, or center of gravity, of the orbiter prior to entry. The other was to give information on the AOS and LOS (acquisition of signal and loss of signal) to the ground stations along the earth trace of the shuttle's orbit. I had to ready these the day ahead and return them to stows for the morning. Tomorrow was the "dress rehearsal," or CDDT, and we had to do it the same way as actual flight.

So it went. I got in very early on that special day, meeting Larry Dunn in our FDF office on the second floor of the O&C building. We were ready! It went smoothly. The crew was up early; they had just finished their breakfast and sauntered into the briefing room. The room filled up quickly. I had the connection with Houston up and they were standing by until the crew was ready. When it was time, I pointed out the changes Larry and I had made to the checklists and turned to the small TV screen connecting with our weather officer in Mission Control. It was all good. The crew was ready. They were anxious to get this show on the road. It was still early. They exited the suite and went down the hall, passing the guard station and walking a little further down the hall adjacent to bonded stows. It was the place where the crew suited up. Two large easy chairs were positioned side by side, one for each of the crew. Support members of the team began assisting the crew with their suits. Even though they were not actually going to fly, they had to prepare as if they were—down to the nth detail.

Having just met with the crew and them now suiting up, I scampered down to stows to retrieve those calculators. I entered the suit room off to the left of where John and Crip were doing their suiting operations and checked out the calculators. They were good. I took both to the crew. John was to have one and Crip was to have the other.

"I'm not going to mess with those things," said Young. "Give those damned things to Crip."

I looked a bit lost because I had been told that John had to have one of them. This was a change. Crip just smiled, and with a shrug took both and inserted them into his leg pockets. He thanked me and I left, wishing them both good luck. The next time I saw them was coming down the hall with their handheld air-conditioning units which attached to their suits. Even though their helmets were still off, this was the configuration they needed. They and a bunch of support personnel went directly to the elevator and descended to the ground floor, where the crew transport van was stationed to take them to Pad 39A. Simulated launch time was almost exactly seven a.m. It would be several hours before that time came. It was early. The entire team was working on adrenalin. It was amazing that even though one knew this was just a rehearsal, the official nature of the exercise made it feel like today was the launch day.

CDDT was a success. Launch and landing scenarios were exercised. Propellants were not loaded. The flight team was ready to go for launch.

It was several days prior to launch. Larry and I had returned again to the Cape and set up our FDF shop. We were ready for whatever we had to do. It was exciting. It almost felt like everything was so well rehearsed that we were getting a bit ho-hum about it—until that day about three days out from the planned day of lift-off. We even had a little time for some beach weather. I took a couple of hours off the day before things were to really pick up. The crew had just arrived and were syncing themselves up for the early wake-up call for the 0700 hours local T-zero time on 10 April 1980. Little did I know that that time in the sun would cause me a great deal of embarrassment.

I had to get to the O&C building around two a.m. on the morning of launch to begin my last-minute support to the crew. The motels in Cocoa Beach were loaded with reporters and tourists from all over the world. I was again in the Polaris—an old motel built when the space coast was in its infancy during the Mercury days. The walls were thin. I tried to get some shut-eye early in the afternoon, and had just nodded off when I heard this loud bunch in the room next door. Apparently, at least one woman and several guys were chugging down some cold ones. They sounded like reporters from England, I think. I could hear everything. I mean everything.

"What if it blows up?" was one person's question. "What do you think the chances are of that happening?"

They continued to discuss the gory likelihood of mission failure and the demise of the crew, and whether they had any protection from any emergency. Little did they know I was listening. I felt like yelling at them. What kind of people were they? I had to get some sleep, but there was no way with all the noise they were making. I got up and went out to the beach, which was a short walk away and down some wooden steps. I needed a break! It was also very crowded, so, feeling trapped, I returned to my room.

The party had apparently broken up, but two people remained, one guy and one gal. What they did next had nothing to do with the shuttle disaster discussion. They banged away like little rabbits. I could hear everything. It was truly X-rated. When they finished I could even hear them in the shower. God, now I really had no interest in sleep, so again I took a short walk. I exited the room only to find that the woman who recently had been in the shower next door was now on the balcony, wearing a robe and drying her hair in the ocean breeze. I passed her on my way to the beach area. We acknowledged each other and I had an overwhelming desire to laugh out loud. I continued my stroll to revisit the beach. I walked down the wooden plank walkway to the steps to the sand. I was hoping the calm of the day would allow me to regain a quiet room for some needed sleep before tomorrow's big day. As I approached the steps I noticed a couple down below lying on a fully reclined beach chaise. What I saw then shook me a bit. He was on his back and she on top, pressed against him. Both wore swimming suits, but she had no top. They were oblivious to the happenings around them. They were making love with their suits on! My God! This was Florida, with ways different from what I was used to—but to do what they were doing! I tried to ignore them, but truthfully, it wasn't easy.

I noticed a family off to the right, parents and two teenage girls between fifteen and eighteen, I guessed. The girls were apparently done for the day and were ready to go back to where they came from. I could hear them; they sounded foreign, but I couldn't place where it might be. The girls were giggling quite a bit. The parents stood and raised a blanket to offer some privacy for the girls to change. Well, it wasn't privacy from my vantage point. Seeing what I saw, and remembering what I had just witnessed, I was in a state of shock. I immediately looked elsewhere and wondered what the hell was going on. This was the day before the launch of the shuttle and I had to get some rest, and had "sex gods" doing everything they could to ensure I would not nod off in a quiet, thoughtless slumber. Oh, well, it was already many days since I had the comfort of my wife and family. I missed them, and especially her. Even more now! I again returned to my room and this time was able to sleep for a bit; a huge surprise, considering the events of the earlier hours.

The morning came—well, it was morning, but the sun was not expected to rise for several hours. I got up, showered, and dressed. Something felt different. *What now?* I thought. I felt a large sore above my upper lip. I somehow had gotten a seriously large cold sore or fever blister on my upper lip. I looked like I had been hit or something. How could this happen so quickly? I was on the beach yesterday afternoon in my free time, but I didn't burn. Reality set in; however, I didn't know what to do about it. It was painful—and getting worse. I finished my preparations and drove to the O&C building. I met Larry as planned.

"What the hell happened to you?" he said. "You look terrible. Someone hit ya?"

"Yeah, I know. I think I got a bit too much sun yesterday," I said.

"Wonder what the folks upstairs are going to say? You know, for launch there are medical folks screening people before they will allow contact with the crew, and you need to be screened."

"Maybe I should get up there sooner rather than later, to work out whatever. If they won't let me in, you will have to do it. The calculators, too!" I said.

I went up and did the thing with the guard, who immediately noticed my fat lip. I thanked him for not commenting. Next, at a table nearby and just in front of the door to the suite was the nurse's station. They looked at me with a very concerned expression.

"What happened to you?" one said. "Let me take your temp."

I explained that I had been in the sun yesterday and this was likely the result. She agreed, but pointed out that this could keep me from getting near the crew. I explained that I was well aware of that, but didn't think I was contagious. She agreed, but required me to wear a mask. I was instructed to leave it on at all times while inside. I took the mask and returned to the FDF office. It wasn't time to enter the quarters yet. Larry was smiling and harassing me about the mask, but I could sense he was also relieved that he didn't have to screw with the weather report or the computers.

It was time to go see the crew. By now they were finished with the traditional prelaunch breakfast and were nearly ready to get on with the briefings and suiting ops. I again went through the badge checks and passed the nurse's station.

"Keep that thing on," she reminded me. Nodding, I assured her I would do as told. Embarrassing as it was, I didn't want this to screw up anything.

I went in. Rick Nygren and a few others were in the gathering. Nearly everyone quizzed me about why I was wearing the mask. God, I felt small. Crip came into the briefing room, looked at me and said, "What the hell is that thing on your face?"

"I got a cold sore. I was told to keep this on as long as I am in here."

"You can't do your job with that on. Take it off."

Feeling somewhat relieved, I removed the mask. "Thank you, sir, I appreciate it," I said. I continued to prepare for the crew's weather briefing. It was iffy; Houston gave a thorough report, as usual. The crew asked them several questions. Deke Slayton, the senior astronaut and the last of the original seven astronauts still working, was standing in the doorway at the other end of the briefing room. Tension was beginning to build in the room. Suddenly, I felt relieved that no one was looking at my swollen lip, but instead was concentrating fully on the mission. This was the day! The weather was questionable in a couple of parameters. Clouds were out there but were expected to clear. The crew had to decide.

"What do you think, Deke?" asked John. I could tell there was a close connection between Deke and the crew. They trusted him.

"Shit, I'd go," he said, and then gave a thumbs-up to the crew, who were sitting on my end of the table. "Enough said. Let's get it on."

The crew and the rest of the group suddenly disbanded. The crew went down the hall, just as they had before, and just as all the other astronauts had in the many years before the shuttle. I followed as before. This time I handed Crip both Hewlett Packard calculators. He smiled. I shook their hands and again wished them luck. I went out in the hallway just outside of the suite and waited along with everyone else. NASA had cameramen there, too. This was going to be an historic event and they were not going to miss it. There was the usual gang of support personnel, as well as NASA management. George Abbey was there, as he always was when the crew was going to fly.

The crew emerged from the suiting room again holding their air-conditioning units, and took the elevator to the ground floor and into the crew van. I took the stairs and arrived to see them just coming out of the O&C building. Entering the van, they both waved to the support group and for the many cameras. I went back into the O&C to retrieve the backup copy of the FDF. I was responsible for transporting that set back to the FAO SSR in the MOCR. It was a duffle bag weighing about sixty-five pounds.

It was 10 April 1981. We were ready and hoped the weather would be, too. It was. The crew was finally on board Columbia and getting into the count. I found a spot outside near the Firing Room to watch. It was as close as they would allow, but closer than the bleachers set up for the special guests. Reporters were like ants everywhere. Political VIPs were everywhere. Loudspeakers were set up for all of us to follow the count.

Everything was going as planned. The weather concern was past and everyone was itching to see the world's newest space vehicle lift off the pad. The count continued. It was nearing the T-ten-minute hold when the team learned that we had a problem with one of the GPCs (general purpose computers). There were five and they all had to communicate back and forth. It was a flight rule. One of them, the BFS (backup flight system), was not in sync with the other four. Time was running short and it looked like we were not going to go. We didn't. At the last minute, the crew was notified of the scrub. At that time, I immediately returned to the O&C building. I had the backup flight procedure. We needed them. It was likely that we would have to recreate some portion of them. It was going to be a long day.

Later that day, Larry and I retrieved from the support crew the Ascent Checklist. We had to update it with new data, just like we had before. We would do it all over again. We had only one problem. When would there be another attempt?

We loitered about until we could get a reading from the experts. Houston was working hard with KSC to understand the problem. We were not sure for many hours what the chances were for a near-term launch. We were told to plan for a nominal forty-eight-hour recycle, in case they could fix the problem. We did just that. Larry and I got some rest and came back to work the FDF later that day. Not much had to be done, but we needed to do some pen-and-ink changes on the Ascent Checklist. John Young was obviously quite upset and extremely disappointed when the scrub was announced. His checklist at the T-ten location was crimped severely and we had to rebuild it. Each flight book was page by page connected with metal rings that were heat-shrink sealed at the clip opening. All of this had to be re-accomplished. I took the old page from John's original flight checklist, and Larry and I fabricated a new one. I kept the old and still have it today. If it had flown it would have been in the Smithsonian.

We were ready. The clock ticked down the hours. We were advised that JSC had fabricated a fix for the GPCs. Effectively, they would update the program and sort of fool the GPCs a bit to maintain agreement. Apparently, the fault was in a timing error that was not clearly understood, but the fix would do the trick. Management bought into it and on we went.

The routine was the same, except this time there were no reporters banging away next door, no beach swimsuit changes, and my lip was healing.

T-zero remained the same, 0700 hours, but the date was the twelfth of April. The team was anxious, but you could see fatigue in their eyes as well. The mission was fifty-six hours long. My direction was to fly back to JSC as soon as possible on the NASA Gulfstream with the backup FDF. I was also to take my position in the FAO SSR with the backup FDF. The flight was planned for somewhere between 0900 and 1000 from the KSC landing strip near the pad.

The count continued. I called Dad in California and told him the latest. We made it past the T-minus-ten hold. The GPCs were talking to each other. There were no leans on the launch. Then, echoing throughout the complex, we could hear: "Columbia, you are go for launch."

"Roger, go for launch," replied John Young. "Looking good from here."

The countdown on the loudspeakers continued: "Ten, nine, eight, we have main engine start…three, two, one, zero. SRB ignition, and we have liftoff of America's first space shuttle." I remember I had tears rolling down my face. I muttered aloud something obscene, too, and gave a mental middle finger to the Soviets. The Cold War was still raging and this was a serious setback for them. We beat them again! I called Dad again and then called my family. Excitement was rampant everywhere. All systems on the orbiter were working nominally. It was all good.

I headed straight for the O&C building, retrieved the FDF bundle, and headed for the strip. My car would be taken care of by others. The airplane was there on the tarmac, waiting. Besides the crew, there were only three of us aboard: me and John's two children, a young girl named Sandy and her brother John. I would guess their ages to be preteen. They didn't talk much. We were in the air soon. It was a short flight back to Ellington AFB—a deactivated base north of Clear Lake City, with minimal services but used by NASA to house many of their aircraft, including this Gulfstream and a fleet of NASA T-38s for astronaut use. There was a ride waiting for me to go to Mission Control (Building 30).

I approached Mission Control and made my way through the maze of security checks. Finally, on the second floor I found my way to the back room to assume my position on console. I opened the door and suddenly all the people in the room stood and applauded. I was completely taken aback and confused. They were on shift the whole time I was at KSC. Many had seen me on CCTV with the crew. To them, I was their link to history at the launch. I was blessed being part of the team that showed the world the might of this glorious nation. I was on the cutting edge of the best of America, my America. It was mine and I was living a dream! The pain of yesteryear's pilot school failure was far in the background. It didn't matter anymore. I was happy.

They were safely on orbit. The mission was going well. We had no real idea how the orbiter would respond to the space environment. We were about to learn a great deal. As part of the routine, one of the first tasks was to open those large payload bay doors. There was no payload in the bay, but the shuttle's thermal control system required the radiators connected to the internal faces of the bay doors to be open to space. If that could not happen the mission would have to be scrubbed. Would the doors open? Would they be so warped from the forces of launch and the thermal extremes that they might stick closed, or maybe not open fully? There were some hitches but the doors came open. Then, the next comment from Crip would stun all of us…

"Houston, Columbia."

"Columbia, Houston, go ahead," responded CAPCOM.

"Just need to tell you we apparently lost a bit of TPS on the starboard OMS pod."

OMS is the Orbital Maneuvering System, the rocket engines on either side of the tail of the shuttle. He gave as much detail as he could, based on what he was able to see from the rear aft flight deck windows. When I heard this coming down and over the loops at Mission Control my heart nearly stopped. I remembered that conversation Crip and I had late at night while working the OMIs. The TPS, he had said, might be the biggest problem; they needed to stay secure or the crew might not survive reentry.

I discussed this conversation with others on console with me in the back room. The idea of losing tiles on the OMS pod didn't bother us so much. They could survive entry if that was all there was. But if they were gone on the OMS pod, where else were they missing? And, if we had knowledge of missing tiles elsewhere, what could be done about it? The short answer was: NOTHING!

I could tell the front room team was working this concern hard. I didn't know it at the time, but later found out that NASA was given support from some of our more secure and secretive government agencies to do whatever they could to assess the threat to the crew. We asked the crew to position the orbiter in a certain attitude and hold until told to change it. They did. Word eventually filtered down that the rest of the orbiter was likely okay. There was no way to be certain. Not yet.

The rest of the mission was nominal. Well, almost! The crew had a newfangled toilet on board that caused them serious angst. We affectionately referred to it as "the slinger." Apparently, the slinger didn't sling. The fecal material was supposed to be able to be separated from the urine through some centrifuge technology. It didn't perform as designed. Nowhere near as designed, in fact. They used the thing, but to their dismay and great disappointment it failed. The crew had particulates of human waste floating all around, necessitating that they reach out with tissues to capture it. Yuck! They ended up resorting to the Apollo method of using stick-on bags, etc. It seems like toilet issues haunted John. During a previous Gemini mission, John was allegedly sickened by a new item on the market called Tang. It was an imitation orange juice. John blamed Tang for his runs. Going to the bathroom in zero gravity was hard enough, but when one got diarrhea it became seriously more difficult. Not just for the victim, but for his crew partners, too. You can imagine. I never had the courage to ask him about it.

The fifty-six-hour mission ultimately came to a successful end. The missing tile concern evaporated once we heard the call from John during entry. Every entry has a blackout, with contact impossible during a short time while passing through the upper atmosphere. This time the short blackout seemed like a million years. Once we heard John's voice, we knew we were good.

Post-mission inspection did reveal some damage, but it was miniscule. The loss of tiles was a great concern. Replacement on orbit was never a possibility. It still isn't.

No one talked about the secret outfit that apparently gave some select NASA personnel information on the tiles. I also did not know then that my life was again about to change, big time, and it had a lot to do with that organization nobody would talk about.

EIGHT

Into the darkness
Questions arise
Answers kept hidden

I continued the support to NASA for the next three missions as I had for the first. My expertise was being honed by those experiences. Engle and Truly—STS-2; Lousma and Fullerton—STS-3; Hartsfield and Mattingly—STS-4; these were the crew members for those next three missions. Each crew was a bit different from the last, but each was great to work with. It was STS-4, however, that propelled my life in much different direction. With the exception of John Young on STS-1, Ken Mattingly was the next most experienced astronaut to fly the shuttle in these early test flight missions.

Although selected as part of the prime crew on Apollo 13, he was removed from that flight because of his alleged exposure to measles, which turned out to be bogus. He did, however, become a key figure on the ground by guiding the Mission Control team on power management of the crippled spacecraft virtually stranded in space, with no clear and immediate ability to return to Earth. His actions contributed enormously to saving that mission from disaster. Ken, apparently being cursed to fly "classified programs," would later be selected as commander for another classified mission designated 51C.

Ken was "blessed" with a pathfinder mission for the Department of Defense (DOD). It wasn't a mission he appreciated very much, but it was a flight. And that is what being an astronaut is all about. He dealt with it. He was instrumental in helping the flight control team to deal with classified shuttle missions. I received a lot counsel from him and Fullerton on how we should create the crew procedures. So, STS-4 was meant to be a test bed for classified shuttle missions because DOD was now becoming an integrated space partner, and I was part of it.

STS-4 was also the end to the predetermined test period of the shuttle program. This decision was wrong and quite premature, but nevertheless NASA hastily decided the program was "OPERATIONAL" after this mission. Today they might regret that decision.

Somehow, the DOD had to learn how to fly classified shuttle programs overtly but protect its classified mission objectives in every way possible. We, both NASA and the DOD, had to learn many new things. The highest levels of government had decreed that the shuttle would be the nation's single access to space. Budgetary reasons forced this flawed line of thinking. NASA had to get used to DOD and move over a bit. It wasn't a popular decision and it was the wrong decision, but it was the directive. It was a shotgun marriage. Working classified in a world used to being nakedly open to the world was indeed a challenge, and my job played a key role in figuring out the answers. The rule was to be open about the mission as much as possible but reveal nothing classified. How the hell do you do that? You can't hide a manned space program requiring thousands of government and contractor people.

We developed a classified procedures development capability. We cleared many with the minimum security clearances so that we had a viable team to create and control the classified data imbedded in the crew procedures. STS-4 was necessary and successful. It proved that we could do it.

Preparations for this mission meant a lot of travel back and forth to a classified location, and many meetings with the crew and the primary payload investigators. We, together, developed techniques to be able to communicate via CAPCOM anything we needed over clear voice nets from Houston direct to the shuttle. The mission team in Mission Control and all the supporting back room teams soon learned a new way of flying a shuttle mission. Future classified missions would require NASA to upgrade its systems from A to Z. It was called controlled mode. Among many security systems upgrades, encryption on all computer systems was put in place. Of the two Mission Control rooms available to control shuttle missions from the Johnson Space Center, the one on the third floor was converted to be able to handle classified programs. I estimated this upgrade to cost the taxpayers at least one hundred million dollars annually.

Indeed, the DOD was fast becoming intimate with the shuttle program. They had many missions to do and the shuttle was their only way of getting them accomplished. It wasn't the best delivery system for our very sophisticated satellites, but orders were orders. The military was *stuck* with the shuttle—a national treasure and an international superstar, but not the right vehicle for what DOD really needed. Instead of expendable boosters, we now had a manned rated vehicle that caused the payload folks to have to deal with man-rating every satellite so that they would not endanger the crew. Not a concern on a throwaway booster. I was extremely proud to be part of the revolutionary shuttle program from the start, but I also doubted that our national leaders knew what they were doing. They had their heads up you know where. Those making decisions for space were not educated in the discipline, and those educated in it didn't have enough political clout to put a stop to the marriage.

Because the DOD was now part of the team, the programs being built in many classified areas of the country had to force their requirements in the shuttle design. Just about the entire vehicle had to be examined and redesigned where necessary. The DOD could not change its national security and highly sophisticated space programs. Because of this mindless decision of our national leaders, NASA was becoming more and more entrapped by the shuttle program, and less and less able to do what it was created to do—explore. The era of Mercury, Gemini, Apollo, and Spacelab was over. Where does the nation go next for space? So, instead of returning to the Moon and going beyond, NASA now had a vehicle that was limited to low earth orbit and could not achieve the orbits that were advertised. I felt stuck in the middle. I loved the shuttle program, but at the same time I understood that marrying DOD with NASA was wrong. NASA also had to return to what it had done during Apollo and go on from there, but budgets and short-sighted planning would force NASA to remain in this rut.

So there we were. The shuttle was it. The DOD was extremely unhappy about it, but had to deal with it. Many in the DOD thought NASA's dedication to the world of classified payloads was not genuine. The lack of trust was deep on both sides. NASA didn't like the dark side and the DOD didn't like the light side. Things were happening behind the scenes to supposedly help this dilemma. My duties within the NASA world were beginning to change.

I was sitting in my office at the Johnson Space Center, working on a new procedure for a future mission, when I received a phone call from a stranger in Los Angeles.

"Major, this is Lieutenant Colonel Larry Glass. I am calling you because of what you do there in Houston, and I am part of an organization that is interested in convincing you to become part of us. We need your skills," he said.

"I'm sorry, sir, but do we know each other?" I asked. "What organization are you referring to?" I was not used to getting calls like this. It sounded unreal to me.

"We are part of Space Division here in Los Angeles. We have an office just formed to manage a new program called the Manned Spaceflight Engineer (MSE) Program. We have thirteen selected officers now and expect to select more in the not-too-distant future. These people are highly talented and motivated. They are all mechanical or electrical engineers and are part of a program which is slated to fly on the orbiter. What you do there is of serious interest to us here. We'd like it if you would agree to fly out for a day or two to meet with us. We can share more with you then. I realize this is all coming at you cold, but if you agree I will work the details to have you come out and visit. We'll be able to talk better face-to-face."

Slightly stunned, I responded, "I need to talk this over with my boss, of course. His name is Colonel Sam

Boyd. Give me a contact number and I will get back to you. You can also call my boss directly if you haven't already done that," I said.

"Thanks. We haven't talked to your leadership yet, but will do so at the right time. By the way, you recently had a meeting with a man named Keith Wright. It was Keith that gave us your name. He thinks you can help. But I think I've said enough for now. Please consider this seriously and get back to us as soon as you can."

He hung up after giving me an office number and a limited organizational description, which left me more confused and wondering what the hell I was getting involved with. I remembered Mr. Wright, but had no clue he was part of a military organization. He wore no uniform when we met; nor did he introduce himself as an Air Force member, just Keith Wright. Apparently, he was in Houston at the center seeking out support for his program—a program he was not privileged to reveal in the open. It turned out that he was an Air Force captain.

I made an appointment with Colonel Boyd. I told him what had just happened with this Colonel Glass. I explained everything I knew to him. He just sat there behind his desk, grinning a bit, which was not uncommon for him. Colonel Boyd was slightly built, sort of skinny, with short hair as expected for a military man. He was a fighter pilot during Vietnam. His assignment to our detachment at the space center was recent, but he seemed to adapt quite well. A friendly guy with a pleasant disposition. He actually became a good friend of mine. He bought a house a few lots down from where I lived in Webster, Texas, and his son became a good friend of our two boys. He pondered a bit. Then he said something that left me wondering what was happening to me and revealed a side of him I had yet to know. Perhaps from one of his prior assignments.

"Well, do you want to take the trip out there?"

"Do you know who they are, sir?"

"Well, let's just say that I am aware. I think it would be good for you to go, but I think you can do something for yourself that may help," he said.

"What's that, sir?"

"Here, let me lend you a book. It's called *The Falcon and the Snowman*. Read it. I don't know if it will aid you, or if it even comes close, but I think you will find it an interesting read. It's new. By the way, if you want to go you can contact this Lieutenant Colonel Glass and tell him to send you TDY orders. It may be good for you to see this place called Space Division for yourself. You know, our parent organization for this detachment is YO within Space Division. When you call him, remind him that your travel and other expenses are his nickel."

"Thank you, sir. Yes, I'll do that. Yes, sir, I knew of our connection with YO. Colonel Lindsay heads that up, I believe, but we here don't see much of him, or anyone from LA. I will contact Glass today," I said, not feeling any surer of what I might be getting involved in.

I hadn't heard of the book, but then it was new, as the boss had said. I was anxious to get into it. I read it cover to cover, but didn't draw the connection between it and the call from Glass. Maybe there wasn't a connection. I called Glass back and told him I had met with my boss, and what the boss had said about funding any travel. He agreed. My TDY orders would be sent soon.

A week later I was in receipt of an authorization to travel to LA. I was to meet in an office within Space Division having the office symbol YOM. It turned out that the organizational chart of Space Division was set up in lettered offices. YOM didn't have any unique meaning—just YOM. My organization in Houston was part of YO, and so was YOM, but I still wasn't too knowledgeable about how Space Division was set up. Since my assignment in Houston, we were more NASA employees than Space Division detachment officers. YOM was an organization within Space Division set up to manage the selected engineers who were charged to work in other satellite program offices. It was a people SPO (Systems Program Office).

I got off the plane at LAX and took the bus to the car rental lot, then drove the three or so miles to Space Division. It wasn't a huge place, sort of stuck there among other office buildings and residential homes. It resembled a college campus. In front of the tallest building for all to see was a full-scale rocket of some kind. Rather symbolic of the mission of the place. This was where the Air Force started in the space business. Satellites and boosters were both funded and engineered from this location. That was the way it had been from the late 1950s to the present.

The buildings were mostly on the perimeter around a central courtyard. It was a bustling little community, teeming with people darting from one building to another. These buildings were filled with military and Aerospace Corporation engineers working various space satellite programs. Many of these programs were going to be lofted into space on the space shuttle. The shuttle experience for these folks was very limited, however. But that was going to change. I had a big role to play in that change.

I found my way to the correct office. It was on the third floor of Building 105, that tall building in the complex with six floors. Suddenly, my path to Glass's office was blocked. I came upon locked double doors with a cipher lock keypad on the wall to the right. Following the instructions posted on the left door, I picked up the receiver of the phone hanging on the wall next to the door and waited. Glass answered the phone and buzzed me in. I pulled on the right door and entered. A man in uniform came into the interior hallway from his office and offered his hand.

"Hello, sir," I said, and introduced myself.

"Hey, hello, and welcome to LA. I'm Larry Glass. Please call me Larry. Come on in and have a chair. Want some coffee?" Larry was a nice enough guy, balding, a bit pudgy for an Air Force officer. He spoke fast and with a manner that gave me the feeling that I already had the job—whatever it was. He came across as a fast-talking dude that was trying to sell me something. I knew nothing of the organization I was visiting, but I had the distinct notion my ignorance would soon disappear.

He continued, "This SPO...you know what an SPO is, don't you?" I acknowledged that I did. "Anyway, this SPO has a unique mission. I cannot divulge everything to you now, but if you choose to become part of our team you will find out. This office was formed at the direction of the secretary of the Air Force, Dr. Hans Mark. He has asked that we go forward with development of a cadre of smart engineers, the MSE program I mentioned to you on the phone the other day. Dr. Mark wants our MSEs to fly on the shuttle as payload specialists for DOD programs and be a fully integrated part of the NASA crew. In short, the secretary has made some high-level agreements with NASA to allow our people to integrate with them and fly with the program, but there it stops. You are the key to make this happen."

"Me? What does all this have to do with me?" I asked. "And by the way, I do have a secret clearance, so if you need to tell me stuff, I am sure my detachment security officer in Houston could verify. Also, is Keith Wright one of your MSEs?"

"I understand and am aware of your clearance level. You will need more. You'll get another special background investigation which is more detailed than that which was done for your current clearance. Yes, Keith is an MSE. He is a captain and is assigned to one of the SPOs. He was in Houston meeting many of the folks you currently work for and with. He learned a lot about you from your NASA counterparts and astronauts. Let me explain a bit of what you would do for us on the staff and for the MSEs. Although we have thirteen selected engineers as our first cadre, they require a lot of stuff to get them on the shuttle. None of them have been trained like astronauts, nor have they been really accepted by NASA as crew members. That will change and you will help in that process. We are on the shuttle—it isn't our desire, but we are here. In case it isn't obvious, NASA and DOD don't see eye to eye, so it is not going to be a piece of cake to move this forward. You would think with the number of military people they have working as detailees they would be friendlier toward us."

"Larry, you probably do not understand where I fit in the NASA world. I am a grunt. A peon! I don't make high-level agreements like those you're taking about. God! I just pinned on major, and these agreements you speak of should be made at the O-6 level or higher. I am not the right guy to get the MSEs to be accepted and integrated on the respective flight crews. I don't know how much you know about how NASA works in the astronaut world, but it's bigger than me. Maybe you should find someone else."

"Oh, slow down. I understand how all this may seem, but don't worry. Let's go down the hall. I want to introduce you to my boss, Colonel Richardson. He can give you more of a sense of where you will fit in here."

We left Larry's office and went down to the other end of the short hallway. Betty, the colonel's secretary, was sitting at a desk just outside the colonel's office. I was introduced to her. She was a nice woman, friendly, slightly heavy-set, with black hair, and old enough to be my mother.

"Hey, there you are, in person. How are you? It's nice to have you here. You know, I must confess, I play a little game when I talk to people over the phone and later meet them. I try to imagine what they look like. I did that with you," she said.

"Well, how did you do? We have had a number of conversations about my orders. Do I fit your thinking?"

"Well, mostly, I had you a pegged as little older, but you're so young-looking." I thought she was buttering me up for some reason. I ate it up, however. "Go on in, the colonel is waiting for you. He's got about a half hour before he has to run off to a meeting across the street."

The colonel was in his office, sitting behind his desk. Small, thin spectacles hung on the tip of his nose. Not a large guy, sort of short and looked like a runner, slightly balding on top, too. Considering Larry's lack of hair, I wondered if this MSE program made people go bald. He looked up, saw me and Larry, and immediately stood. With a smile, he invited us in and asked us to sit down.

"Hello," he said, offering his hand and grinning. "Well, what do you think? Are you going to join us here?"

"Well, sir, I am not sure. All of this is a surprise to me. I am not sure I am the man for the job."

"Please call me Dave. We sure have heard a bunch of great news about you and what you have done in Houston, and how you worked with the crews for the first few missions," he said. "Your involvement in the crew training branch there and the crew procedures world is impressive—and for us, crucial. You also apparently have a deep trust within the astronaut corps."

"Thank you, sir," I said. "I don't know your sources about my work at the space center, but yes, I have come a long way in a very short two years down there. I was honored to be put in front of the flight crews and be part of the Mission Control team. But…"

"But what?" he said.

"Well, from what Larry told me, you want me to help obtain agreements with NASA on the MSE payload specialist program, train them, etc. I am not sure I am the right level for that, sir." I tried to be honest. I didn't want these strangers to think I was someone I wasn't. I was a working dog at the Johnson Space Center, a trainee myself, and they wanted me to make magic happen.

"Relax, Major, perhaps Larry overstated your involvement with all that. Our boss, Major General Kulpa, has already worked out with Secretary Mark and the folks at NASA headquarters a lot of these agreements—MOUs and such. Perhaps the folks at the lower levels in NASA haven't been informed yet, but they will be. Nevertheless, your help is critical to us. You are the right guy, trust me!" He went on describing where Secretary Mark and General Kulpa intended to go with the MSE program. Military man in space was his catch-phrase. "By the way, I briefed the general about you. In time, you will meet with him, too. He is eager to get to know you."

My mind was zinging around like an out-of-control toy top. I was getting excited listening. Apparently, the Air Force was not only going to have a "blue" shuttle, we were going to have our own payload specialists; people to fly with the program that lived with it from the cradle. They would be our on-orbit experts.

What Larry and Dave didn't say in our meeting was something I already knew. Although not true down to the typical engineer and the workers, NASA didn't like DOD and DOD had trust issues with NASA. The DOD wasn't convinced that NASA would be available to get to know the program well enough in advance of the mission to fully understand the technical aspects as well as the mission aspects for that hardware. There were two very different cultures. There was distrust to the bone—on both sides. I enjoyed my time in Houston and the trust the NASA team showed me, but now, with this new duty with the MSEs, I was fearful that I would be cast aside as some sort of traitor. My fears were just that—fears—and not reality. My bonds with the people I worked with were strong. For that I was grateful. But now, I was seeing both sides of the issue.

It didn't make any difference that the astronauts were mostly from military backgrounds; many were still on active duty but detailed to NASA. They were NASA, not DOD, and we couldn't force them to come into the payload world to the level we thought we needed. Hence, the reason for the MSE program! It was true that NASA routinely came across as more concerned about its image politically than meaningful science. Our astronauts were used—no, correction— underused. Great minds, great bodies, eager, etc., but NASA management kept telling them to play the game of public relations. They were sales representatives. Ah, but I digress...

I returned to Houston with a new vision and lots of thoughts of where I was likely to go with this new assignment, knowing that they asked me, not the other way around. They found me! Needless to say, I wanted the job! Reflecting back to those days in pilot school and then in the ICBM business, and even further back to that little place where I grew up, it was difficult for me to grasp how all this was made possible. All the changes in my life, but each time the career course changed it was always with rockets and man in space. It sort of made one believe in predestination. This was yet another opportunity to reveal to my family a new role I would play for man in space. This time, it was military man in space to me. I had rubbed elbows with the giants of our nation's space program and been awed that it happened. I now had a new assignment that would yet again reveal to me new horizons, places our government created but kept hidden from most of the world, and I was to become a part of it. A "classi-fied" space program!

My new clearance was processed and I was briefed. I wasn't overly impressed with my new knowledge. I cannot reveal in this book all that was told to me. I am still denied the opportunity to tell everything I know, and I fear that rule will remain with me the rest of my life. What I can tell the world is that this new mission was—and is still today—a very significant period for our nation's space program. It had its good and bad sides. I hope I will be remembered as being on the good side. I think I was.

With the new assignment, I had great support from NASA management as well as from my military supe-riors and friends, but I couldn't say a word about what I was going to be doing. Much of it was still unknown to me.

Another great motivator to accept the new job was that we really wanted to get out of Houston. Its weather was designed for the unenlightened or the trapped. God, it was bad! I did the same routine of house hunt-ing, but this time we got a temporary rental so that my dear wife could have a clear vote and I would stay out of trouble. I had learned my lesson. Next place—she picks! And she did.

Eventually we settled in our new place and the fam-ily liked it. The boys had to make new friends again, and like the wonderful sons they are, they did just that. Certainly, as with all the other moves we had made, they missed the buddies they left behind. They came to like their new home in a bedroom community forty-five miles from my LA office in YOM. My wife found her way around, too. She liked the new home she picked!

I was discovering more of my responsibilities in this new Air Force Manned Spaceflight Engineer program. At first there were thirteen chosen, but that number would increase to twenty-seven during my watch, and more even later. My job was to train them, integrate them into the NASA world, and set up a selection process for flight. I was being fully integrated into this military man in space, and I loved where all this could potentially take us—the DOD. In fact, after only two weeks on the job my boss asked me to come see him about a challenge he had for me.

"Yes, sir, what's up?" I asked. It was a very casual office and we didn't stand on a lot of military formalities. After Dave asked how I was getting the feel for my new job, he sprang it...

"I want you to do me a favor. I realize you are pretty new here, but I want you to fly to Washington next week. I was supposed to give a briefing on military man in space to a large group of industrial and government bigwigs, but I can't make it. General Kulpa has me doing something else right on top of this. I need you to give my briefing for me. It's at the Xerox Training Center just outside of DC."

"But—"

"Yes, you're right for the job. It will be a snap."

"But, sir—"

"You'll have to fly out the day ahead. I had a place reserved at a hotel right across from the Pentagon. You can see Glass; he'll take care of any questions you can come up with. God, it's good to have you aboard."

"But, sir—"

"Sorry, I don't have a lot of time right now to discuss it. I gotta go across to the other side, got a meeting with a bunch of folks. See Larry. You'll do fine."

"Yes, sir." *Okay*, I thought, as I left his office and returned to mine, *after just two weeks, I have to give a briefing to about three hundred doctoral experts and corporate VIPs on something about which I know virtually nothing.* I had to get to Larry ASAP!

"Ah, so how do you like your new job? Fun, ain't it? We've got a lot of work to do and we are terribly understaffed. Your being here is a big help. But that ain't why you're here now, is it. What's up?"

"Larry, I just got set up by the boss. Do you have any idea what he just told me? He wants me to give a detailed pitch to a bunch of cheeses on military man in space. Like I am an expert. He wants me to go next week." I must have looked like I was in a state of shock.

Larry just smiled. "Well, welcome to the MSE program. I have his charts. Here, take this and go over them, and if you have questions maybe I can help. Oh, I currently plan on going, too, but you will prime and be the briefer. So, my advice is, get used to it. You are now an expert! Again, welcome aboard. Seriously, it will be a good opportunity for you."

I took the package and went back to my desk. God, there were about a hundred slides! Lots of stuff I had heard about, but not much detail. Larry and I—and Dave, too, when I could catch him—discussed the briefing in as much depth as was possible.

Finally the day came. I took the only flight I could that would get me into DC at a reasonable time. I was as ready as I could possibly be. My next challenge was to understand the layout of DC and get to my hotel, and research the maps to find the Xerox Center.

As luck would have it, I was so nervous about being set up to brief all these experts that I couldn't sleep at all the night before. I knew I had to get some sleep, but it didn't happen. I probably got two hours total. *Good*, I thought, *I'll likely fall asleep during my pitch.*

It was early the next day. The weather was great, and I soon found myself on the freeway headed for someplace I had never been before. The rental car was okay, but stunk with a mix of cigarettes and cheap perfume. Yuck! Washington, DC. God, what a place! Confusing highways, traffic even worse than LA, and the way the roads were set up seemed like a plot by the founding fathers to confuse future inhabitants. I was sure I would not get through this without some major screwup. I looked up ahead—ah, there it was. God, what an impressive complex, but where do I park? Okay, good, there were signs.

My serious lack of sleep hadn't impacted me much, yet. I was working on pure adrenaline and that was a good thing. I parked the car, got out, and found my way into a huge room that was rapidly filling up. I noticed the presenters had small tables with assigned names. Yup, I found my name. One of the hosting officials came up to me, introduced himself, and gave me instructions on filling out my name tag. I looked around for Larry—no Larry. Hell, I had to give this flying solo. Thinking that word "solo" gave me an immediate flashback to several years prior. I remembered the vow I took—not to screw up the next challenge. So, I took a deep breath, went over to the refreshment table, and got something that would suffice for breakfast. More importantly, I found the coffee. I had started to give myself a caffeine transfusion when I heard a familiar voice—Larry's.

"Ah, you made it," I said. "Well, I'm as ready as I ever will be. Take a look, Larry, there are hundreds of them. Some even look foreign. Have you seen the list of people that are to present? These folks are real experts, top pedigree, PhDs, etc." Just then, I realized I was rattling on. I was nervous and he knew it.

"Well, I finally got out of the traffic jam and made it here just in time," he said. "The way I look at it is that we are here to introduce an opportunity for others to learn a bit from us on where our country might like to go in space. We obviously cannot divulge our classified side, but we can generate a lot of discussion. You will brief, and if there are questions you can't answer, perhaps I can. Bottom line: don't lie. We either know it or we don't, and we cannot comment on the stuff we know we can't tell them, right?"

"Well, I am glad you're here. Oh, look, it appears they are getting organized. This is likely to be a long day. At least they have me up earlier rather than later. Should be able to get it done before lunch." Larry agreed.

The meeting was called to order and the preliminary speeches by the hosts were made. I thought that if I weren't a presenter I might actually enjoy this thing. I listened to the depth of the briefings made by others. They had their feces consolidated. They really were experts.

Then I heard the host say, "And next up, we are privileged to have with us a speaker from the Air Force, Space Division, in Los Angeles. He will speak on the military man in space. It should enlighten us all."

My stomach muscles began to tighten. It was suddenly my turn. I heard the exploding sound of applause. *God*, I thought, *applauding BEFORE I speak. I wonder if they will feel the same when I am done.* I got up and went to the stage. I did a little covert inspection of my uniform; good, barn door zipped! I began my—DAVE's—presentation.

It was easier than I thought; either that or I was so tired I didn't know it when I screwed up. Knowing there were a lot of egghead elites from NASA, I opened my remarks commending NASA on its achievements and giving some of my personal experiences while in the shuttle program. That got applause, making me feel bolder to press forward with the rest of the briefing.

Then it was over, and after a few well-placed questions from numerous members of the audience, I felt that I had been successful. More applause was bestowed on me. I thought they actually were being polite. Maybe they were clapping because I was done. I thanked them for the opportunity and left the stage to go back to my table. As soon as I sat down, I had an overwhelming sense of tiredness come over me like a black sheet. I feared I would nod off, but didn't. During the breaks a lot of those eggheads approached me and Larry to squeeze us for more information. Not a problem for me, I had none.

As it turned out, the opportunity to give that presentation shaped me for future tasks, and I was grateful. A few weeks later I received a package in the mail from the host of the conference. It was a package of all the presentations. The enclosed letter said it was their intent to print a bunch and send them out to others on their list, and if I objected to please notify them. I checked with my boss—his reply was, "Go for it. You are now published." I laughed and left his office, and after returning to mine I responded to the enclosed letter.

The MSE program kept me traveling and very busy. I was learning the ropes and a hell of a lot about our military space programs. I was a true believer in what we were doing or going to do in space. I, too, believed at the start that the DOD and NASA were like vinegar and oil. I was, at the time, convinced that we really had a reason to have our representative on orbit with the crew. We had many planned DOD shuttle missions in the near future. None of the MSE activity thus far enabled any common understanding with NASA. They were still apprehensive about flying anyone that wasn't an astronaut, although they had future plans to fly civilians. It was the DOD versus NASA. We in the MSE program had a serious uphill battle to win NASA over. As I said, I was a believer, a good soldier, and I thought the program was necessary. The MSEs were selected from a wide range of officers to carry the DOD flag in this new era of manned spaceflight. We all knew they were not astronauts, although eventual public documentation in the press would call them that. Of course, NASA certainly didn't agree with those publications.

However, in order to convince the management in Houston that the MSE program was real and intent on fulfilling its task, I had to set up a rigid training program and a scoring method which would withstand doubting scrutiny and convince NASA that our payload specialist would be not a hindrance but an asset to the mission.

The training was multifaceted and expensive. With the help of the Navy, we developed a two-week program—a portion of the Navy SEAL training program in San Diego. It was all physical and damned hard on the MSEs. I should point out that the real SEALs were not impressed. We were intruding into a very hallowed area. We also made agreements with NASA at Marshall Spaceflight Center in Huntsville, Alabama, to use its Water Immersion Facility for space suit familiarization. We made arrangements at the Edwards Air Force Base Flight Test Center (AFFTC) Test Pilot School to fly the MSEs in a series of demanding T-38 flights as backseat flight test engineers. The AFFTC put each of them through a series of very tough rides, with specific objectives to accomplish while flying in various scenarios. Next, we flew the MSEs for several flights in NASA's "vomit comet" for parabolic flights to simulate weightlessness while accomplishing defined tasks. Yes, they don't call it the "vomit comet" for nothing. The MSEs got their share of airsickness. Astronauts don't get airsick; fifty percent of them, however, get "space adaptation sickness." It's the same thing. Finally, we submitted them to a flight physical that far surpassed NASA's. The physical was done at the Brooke Army Medical Center in San Antonio, Texas. It included both physical and mental assessment. Yup! All of our MSEs were physically fit and—believe it or not—sane! We did all these things and more. We disclosed our efforts and, as required, the detailed results to NASA management. We were not giving in. We wanted to be part of the crew and were determined not give NASA any chance to say no.

The satellite programs were maturing and their planned mission dates were approaching. Time was running short to get our MSEs assigned to those missions. Most of that effort fell on me and one or two of my assistants. We were ready to select the MSEs for flight assignments and tell NASA our decisions.

It fell on my shoulders to go forward with a process. I didn't have a real plan, but the generals I worked for needed it done. I discussed all of this with my immediate bosses. They put it back on me. One Friday, after much thought and several discussions with a few of my co-workers, I went home for the weekend. I decided I had to give it my best shot. What I did next would impact the entire MSE program, as well as ultimately force NASA to deal with the MSEs.

It was early morning and I decided to sit down in the living room before my family got out of bed. I needed to get my thoughts together. In about an hour, I ended up creating selection criteria that eventually would have to be bought by my immediate staff and our general officers. It was tough but fair.

I took my criteria to the generals and one by one got them to agree. Besides NASA, the MSE program was not overly popular with my general bosses, either—they didn't necessarily believe in its goals. The program was put in place by the secretary of the Air Force, Dr. Hans Mark. The generals had to live with it. So did the rest of us. I was still convinced we were onto something, and so were all of the MSEs. They were eager to fly, perhaps at the expense of loyalty to their respective programs. In that regard they reflected the same viewpoint as did the astronauts. The difference, however, was that the astronauts were picked specifically to fly in space—our MSEs weren't. None of them were specifically promised a flight, only a strong likelihood. Nevertheless, we all proceeded with a selection ranking as if each MSE would fly at some point in the future. The generals all agreed that the criteria I had created were good and would work. I was ordered to create a selection package tailored after a general officer selection board protocol, and to set up a time for all to convene and consider the packages.

The MSEs were already assigned to the various program offices, with typical engineering duties. They were to learn the program and contribute whatever they needed to as legitimate members of the program offices. All were trained about the shuttle and its technical interfaces. Their job was to work these interfaces. They traveled back and forth to the space center in Houston a lot, and often worked with actual flight crew members. All were smart and motivated. But now it was time to reassess, choose primary and backup for the missions, and inform NASA.

It's amazing how dear a friend I became to many of them when they found out what I had to do in this selection process. They were all sucking up. But I warned them that I had a job to do and they were to keep their distance. I knew I had to keep the entire process secret. In fact, I was ordered by the generals to keep it under wraps. It was to be kept between me and a couple of others from YOM and the generals, and they knew it. I kept my office door locked any time I left. However, one day...

"Hey, good morning. This is your favorite general, General Kutyna. Get your ass over here now, we need to talk."

I was stunned. The general didn't call us, we called him. What the hell was going on? It was a little past 0700 hours, and something very important had to be happening in order for the boss to cancel his morning briefings.

"Yes, sir, I'm on my way."

I was at the general's door in less than two minutes. I knocked.

"Enter. Okay, Major." I tried to salute like a formal reporting, but he ignored it. "Sit down. What the hell are you doing with those MSE packages? I thought we told you to keep those selection folders and the process protocol to yourself!" he said. The general was pissed and I didn't know why.

"But I have, sir," I replied. "May I ask what this is about?"

"Last Friday, just about happy hour at the club, one of your MSEs was blowing in my ear—sucking up, I expect. I didn't appreciate it, but she mentioned something about the selection process that only you and a few others are aware of. What she said told me implied she had seen the packages. Now, Major, how the hell does that happen?"

Now I was getting pissed. How could that possibly be the case? I always locked my office door and the file cabinet containing the folders. I was lost.

"Sir, I don't know." I explained how I handled the packages. I emphasized that it would be impossible for a person to casually see the contents of the folders. They would have to try.

"Look, I don't care how it happened, that's your job to figure out, but I will not tolerate this type of thing happening again. This whole goddamned MSE program is creating more headaches than it's worth. I expect my staff to do the right thing. Is that clear, Major? Now get out of here and go fix this problem."

"Yes, sir," I said. I saluted and assured him that he would never have this problem again. At the same time, my mind was in overdrive. I knew who he was referring to as blowing in his ear. Only one person of my group would fit. I had only two female MSEs. One was happily married; she would be the last to play up to the boss. It had to be Charlene. She was single but had been married once; not a dummy, but suffered from a bit of an ego problem. After what the general had put me through, I was pissed. I had to get to the bottom of it. I returned to my office and placed a call, ordering her to my office ASAP.

A short time later there was a knock at my open office door. "You wanted to see me, sir?" The captain stood in the doorway with a smirky grin on her face. However, it faded fast after she noticed the not-so-happy look on mine.

"Yes, Captain, please come in and sit down. I want Lou in here with us." I called next door for Lou to join us. He came in looking confused and sat down.

"Sir, what's up?" Lou wanted to know more. I hadn't had a chance to fill him in, so he was about to hear everything for the first time.

"Well, maybe Charlene can help us a bit," I said. "Captain, were you at the O Club last Friday around happy hour time?"

She looked confused and said that she had been, and wondered why I cared. I responded by telling her of my early morning encounter with the general. I gave her and Lou the details of my meeting. The captain was fidgeting in her chair.

"Did you have an opportunity to talk with General Kutyna last Friday?" I asked.

She looked very uncomfortable. "Yes, we danced a bit. He's not a good dancer, though."

"What did you discuss with the general?"

"Well, nothing much."

"Specifically, Captain, did you discuss anything related to the selection process we have ongoing?"

"Well, I did mention the process that you are running, but that was all."

I could tell there was more. "Look, I was called this morning almost as soon as I put my ass in this chair. It was Kutyna, referring to himself as my favorite general and telling me to get my ass down to his office. What he told me was something I didn't quite know how to handle. One of my MSEs was blowing in his ear—and that's a direct quote, Captain. The general went on to explain that what this MSE told him was information she could not know unless I divulged it to her. Now, I ask you, did you tell the general anything? And if you did, what did you tell him and how did you get the information?" My anger was apparent and she knew it. Lou just looked at me, probably wondering how the rest of the day might go.

"Well, Major, I don't blow into anyone's ears, and I am telling you I couldn't have said anything I don't know about. I have never been in your office when you weren't here. I also didn't see any of the records you are creating for the selection process. Sure, I am curious, but not enough to snoop."

I could tell she was on the defensive. I also knew I couldn't prove anything, one way or the other.

"Okay," I said. "Let me advise you to stay away from the general socially. I don't know why the general feels so strongly, but he does. I only know what he said to me about your conversation last Friday. I am not going to do battle with the general. I take orders, just like you. If what you said is true, the general might be overreacting. He obviously thought you knew something you shouldn't. Look, I am willing to let this go, but I need you and the rest of the MSEs to understand that this is not a small deal and it's not fun for me. We are doing something here that was never before done and it's an uphill process. The pressure is up and it ain't going away anytime soon. It's a political thing, and not just with us on the staff, or you and your MSE counterparts, but with NASA as well. I hope you understand what is happening here. You are dismissed."

She left quickly and, I fear, a little pissed. Too bad!

"Sir, what the hell happened this morning?" asked Lou, clearly at a loss.

I understood his confusion. I explained in detail how my morning had gone and how pissed the general was. I also told him that I hadn't wanted to meet with Charlene without a witness. And I didn't want to be called by the general again.

The day soon came for the general officers to convene and select a number of MSEs for flight with the various programs being readied to fly the orbiter. I had all the folders ready and delivered to the top floor of Building 105, the commander's suite. We were to convene with the four general officers in the conference room. The ranking general was a three-star, the Space Division Commander. Next was a two-star, and two one-star generals. They all kept their schedules free for several hours that day. I positioned the files in front of them and left the room. I was to be notified when they were finished. It took about three hours. I got a call from the sixth floor.

"Major, this is General McCartney's secretary. They have completed their selections. They are ready for you to come back to conference room now." I knew who she was and also understood that she knew the pressure I was under. I left immediately for the elevator.

I reported in typical military fashion. The room smelled a bit stale. They obviously had had a lot of long conversations about not just the selection process, but perhaps the worthiness of the entire MSE program they had been given to govern. I was given the results of their selections. I was told that they had selected a prime and a backup MSE for each of the five programs coming up. Which MSE that would ultimately fly was still to be decided—another selection would be made as needed for each mission. That meant another process like the one we had just gone through, but simpler.

The first was mission coming up was STS 51C. They selected Keith Wright and Gary Payton to work that program. Actually, Keith and Gary were already working in that program office, but this action made their position official.

The common belief among many of the MSE peers and some of the staff was that Keith was technically more familiar with the payload than Gary and would be the better choice to actually fly, but something Ken Mattingly, NASA's selected crew commander for 51C, had said to me would influence the down selection. Ken and the rest of the crew flew to the West Coast many times while preparing for the mission. Keith and Gary attended all of the sessions, and I could sense the competition between them. Both had been working with the selected crew even prior to this time, so they actually knew each MSE quite well.

During a short break in one of our technical meetings in the program office, Ken came up to me. He was concerned about one of our MSEs actually becoming more of a problem than a source of a solution.

Ken said, "I'm not going to try to tell you what to do here, but it would really help if you considered and weighted your decision heavily in the direction of whether the MSE is rated." I knew where he was going—it would float a lot better if the one we chose to fly on his mission was a pilot. We had two, Major

Gary Payton and Captain Bill Pailes. If we went with Ken's "recommendation," I could see that it would be virtually impossible to fly any of the non-pilot engineers. I later met with my general officer bosses and discussed the Mattingly comments regarding being a pilot versus not. They never admitted to me how they felt. Whether they agreed with Ken or not was unknown to me. I did have to consider the NASA comment, though, in the criteria for down selection I had to create, and did.

Keith was never told that that was the deciding factor, regardless of the superior technical knowledge of the program he possessed over Payton. Payton was selected to fly STS 51C. The mission flew successfully on 24 January 1985. Major Payton contributed well to the mission and was promoted to lieutenant colonel, effective immediately upon landing, as was typical at the time for first-time military space flyers. It was called a presidential promotion.

Captain Pailes would be selected to fly on STS 51J. It was launched successfully on 3 October 1985. Pailes and Payton turned out to be the only MSEs ever to fly on the shuttle. The fact that they were pilots was a big bonus. When Pailes flew he was a major selectee—his pin-on date was very close to his mission flight date. When he landed, he also received a promotion. He went from captain to lieutenant colonel in record-breaking time.

The MSE program continued as it had, with all still thinking they had a chance for flight. The struggle with NASA continued. I, too, was having a problem dealing with the reason for the MSE program. Prior to the Challenger accident the program struggled for support—both internal and external. I personally challenged the cadre to come up with serious reasons why they had to fly with their program. I never got a good answer and I couldn't think of any, either. I initially thought as they did: they had to for mission assurance reasons. I was wrong!

The MSEs were beginning to get the idea that they had been duped into an LA assignment just to enhance the program offices, under the guise of flying on the shuttle. They understood that our senior leadership was no longer supportive of the program. To them, the program was more trouble than it was worth. I understood how each of the MSEs must have felt. I left to go on an overseas assignment in February 1985, which was after 51C but prior to 51J. I was therefore overseas when the Challenger accident happened on 28 January 1986.

In addition to the pressures created by the Challenger accident, the program was flawed from the beginning. The MSE program could never justify why it was needed. Dr. Hans Mark was no longer the secretary of the Air Force. It became Mr. Pete Aldridge, and I daresay he was a tepid supporter. He didn't like the program because it was too political and it didn't make any real technical sense. There was no proof that the MSE would provide mission assurance beyond what the normal astronaut crew would provide.

The MSE program would soon come to an end. The selected MSEs rightfully felt screwed. They were promised things the Air Force could not make happen. A program based primarily on lack of trust and fighting between government agencies was wrong. But that was the way it went. I felt duped as well.

Over time, the DOD learned to fly on the shuttle in a classified way, but not with any MSE on board. The

Challenger accident also forced decisions to allow the DOD to get back to the expendable rockets. The entire experience of the shuttle was good for all, but we made mistakes. Lots of them!

NINE

To the far side of Earth
Next stop, Down Under
Challenges

The drone of the engines didn't allow for sleep. I knew I should try, but my thoughts and the noise didn't let it happen. It was going to be a long flight. They said it was fifteen hours to Sydney. I had thirteen to go. It was nearly midnight when we left LAX. The elderly couple sitting next to me was asleep, the woman with her head against the window and the man in the middle seat, head back and mouth wide open—snoring. I guess when you're older it's easier. Surely, I deserved first or business class; nope, I had an aisle seat in "swill" class directly across from the toilet.

It was the thirteenth of February when we took off, already it was the fourteenth, and when we crossed the date line it would be tomorrow. Our younger son's birthday was the fourteenth. When the plane landed in Australia it would be tomorrow, the fifteenth. How did that work? Thankfully, we had celebrated his birthday yesterday.

This was not just going to be a long plane ride but a long tour as well. I was a major in the United States Air Force. I had just left behind my beautiful wife and our two great sons. I had to go this trip alone. I would be gone fifteen months. The wrenching angst in my heart and gut just thinking of being away from them for so long hurt. We had discussed the options long and hard and this was the only way. If I refused the assignment, my career would be over. If I took them with me, it automatically would turn into at least a two-year tour, and that was too long to uproot them. The boys were settled in our new place in Simi Valley; they liked their school and were doing well in it. My wife had a good job near home and she, too, would sacrifice if she left. Then, what would we have done with the home we just bought? The Air Force didn't care. If they wanted you to have a family they would have issued you one, or so the saying goes. Anyway, there I was, and I had to deal with it. One good thing about it—Kangaroos didn't carry weapons. My buddies that went to Vietnam were dealt a different set of cards. I preferred the Kangaroos!

Then there was my dad. That wonderful man who stepped into the picture to complete the job of another many years ago. That great man who gave me his last name and taught me how to handle the challenges of life. The man who loved to drink a beer and smoke a cigar while talking with me about everything from anthills to aliens. The man who would wake me up in the middle of the night, only to drag me outside in the snow and cold to show me the heavenly displays of stars and the comets flying through them. That man who I called my best friend was dying. He was struck by cancer and thought he had beaten it, but that wasn't going to be...

"Hi, Dad, how do you feel today?" I thought, *what a stupid question*. There he lay, in bed; the cancer had already taken his eyesight and his ability to even get up without help. He was hardly able to form the words when he spoke. But he was awake and aware. His cancer was tough. It slowly ate away until the vital organs could not do their job. The future...well, there wasn't any future, just the waiting until death came. He was sixty years old.

"Well, I'm doing," he said. "Not a whole lot that I can do. Mom does her best taking care of me." Mom was a nurse and was able to give him the drug doses to keep the pain down. It was a tough job. She had to wash him, take care of his bathroom needs, and all that. She also had to continue to work at the local Oceanside hospital in order to maintain insurance coverage. She got help from others to sit with Dad while she had to be gone. Not much of a life for her, either. They lived about three hours away from us and we tried to see Dad as much as possible. I really loved talking to him.

"Son, just be glad you're not my real son," he said. I knew what he meant, but I hated those words. He WAS my real dad—hell, he even learned to call me something besides Bub, and I learned long ago how to spell my new last name. Yup! He was my real dad. Cancer ran in his genes—that was what he meant.

"Dad, I came down to see you one more time be-fore I leave for Australia. It's a long assignment and I don't want to leave you like this, but I really haven't got a choice," I said, with tears welling up and my voice quivering.

"When do you ship out?" he asked.

"Well, I have to be in Woomera on the sixteenth. I leave here from LA on the thirteenth, in just a week. This is the only time I had to come down to see you."

"I appreciate that, son. Don't worry about me. You have your life to live. But remember this,"—he reached out for my hand and with a heavy breath continued—"I will be there in Australia before you get back home."

After that comment, I could hardly say the words. "Good attitude, Dad, I'll be there waiting for ya. Don't forget what you said." I gave him a hug and kissed his forehead. "Good-bye, Dad. I love you."

"I love you, too. See you soon, son. Fly safe, and tell the family I love them, too. I'll be in Australia before you get back," he said.

Those words stuck with me. I changed my thoughts to something a bit lighter. I still wasn't tired. My seat neighbors were out. The snoring was funny. I couldn't have slept with that going on even if I were tired. At least he wasn't leaning on my shoulder. I picked up my new book to pass the time.

"Well, how are you doing, sir? Can I get you anything? Water, soft drink, or something with a bit more spike?" the flight attendant asked. She was doing her rounds. Most of the passengers were trying to sleep, so she and the others were quietly going up and down the aisles to see what they could do for those of us still awake.

"Thanks, water would be nice."

"What's the book, interesting?"

"Yeah, it's by James Michener, called *Space*. Turns out that I know a lot of the folks mentioned in the book. It is classified fiction, but based on truth," I said.

"Here's your water. What do you mean, you know a lot of the characters?" she asked.

"Well, I'm an Air Force major, actually a lieutenant colonel selectee, and I worked in Houston at the Johnson Space Center. I was fortunate enough to be given duties for direct support to the astronaut crews on the first four space shuttle missions. I got to know a lot of the space heroes personally. I also remember when Michener came to the space center preparing for his book." I took my water and set it on the tray.

"Sounds like you have had an interesting career. You know, I shouldn't say this, but we have an astronaut on board with us tonight." She looked like she had just violated a code of conduct by telling me that.

"Really, who?"

She stammered a bit, but eventually said, "Alan Shepard. He's in business class, seat 14B."

"You've got to be kidding me. Alan Shepard, our first astronaut to see space in Mercury." I was taken completely aback. *I have to meet him,* I thought.

"Nope, I'm not kidding. I don't know if he would appreciate being bothered. But if you decide to meet him, you didn't hear it from me."

I understood. It took a bit of courage, but I finally decided to take the chance and go forward. I hoped he would be awake and willing to shake my hand. Wow! This was some ride. I went from grieving about my dad, missing my family, and putting up with an old man snoring just inches away from my right ear to a feeling of excitement at possibly meeting our nation's first astronaut. This was Providence. I decided to go for it. I left the book on my seat pocket and got up.

The fasten seat belt light was off and I needed to get up and stretch anyway. I nudged forward past the toilet and galley and sought out the left side of the plane for row 14. Aha, there it was. There he was. He was sitting in the aisle seat with a woman I presumed to be his wife on his left, near the window. They both appeared to be awake. I took that as a good sign and approached.

"Good evening, sir." He looked up, probably wondering who the hell I was and what was so good about the evening. I gave him my name and said, "I think we have a few friends in common."

"We do? Like who?" He was pleasant, and so was his wife beside him.

"Well, like Deke Slaton, John Young, Bob Crippen, and a few others," I said. "I worked the first four shuttle missions in crew procedures development and gave direct support to them. They were great to work with and I learned a lot."

Shepard looked more interested in what I was saying after I dropped a few names. We chatted a little with me crouching down next to his seat. He introduced his wife. She was a kind lady, and her expression made it clear that she had been through this kind of stuff before. It was late and I knew he must have been tired. We were drawing a crowd, and I didn't think he would like his presence made known to the entire airplane, so I apologized.

"Ah, that's alright, I'm used to it by now." We talked more of my duties in Houston. He was impressed.

"You know, Mr. Shepard, I don't know how to say this, and I'm not trying to make you feel old, but when you flew the first time I was in civics class in my freshman year of high school. I was so moved by what you were doing that I actually patterned my life in space and space-related areas. I have been very lucky. Meeting you adds just more icing to the cake, and I appreciate it."

"Well, Major, it has been a true pleasure to have met you, too. We have a lot in common—not just the friends, but the spirit of our connected careers. Keep up the good work and good luck to you." I thanked him and left.

As soon as I got back to my seat I resumed reading my novel. Then it suddenly occurred to me. *Shit. I should have taken the book with me.* I fidgeted in my seat, thinking I had to do something about it. I did.

"Excuse me one more time, Mr. Shepard. I wonder, would it be too much to ask of you to sign my new book by Michener? It's titled *Space.* You're in it, as you likely know." I felt a bit embarrassed, but it was worth it.

"Sure, give it here." He took the book and signed it. Just a simple good luck and a signature. That book remains as a very treasured item in my library today, as it would in any library.

I don't know the reason for his trip, but it was probably business. Even before he left NASA he had become very wealthy from his business pursuits. Our country's first man in space and the world's second—the Soviets beat us with Yuri Gagarin.

With the headwind we couldn't quite make it direct to Sydney, so we were told that we would land in Fiji for more fuel. Not a big deal, but it would allow us to get off the plane. That toilet immediately to my left reeked after such a long flight. I hoped they would take care of that, but they didn't! We got our short break and then back on board.

We finally landed and cleared customs in Sydney. I had no idea of where to catch my next airplane. I was able to get some directions from one of the officials. I just had to take a short bus ride to an adjacent terminal. I was tired but had to press on. I was soon on the plane to Adelaide, where I was to meet my sponsor. They always give a new person a sponsor to help him or her learn the ropes. Mine was supposedly waiting for me at the airport. I had no idea what he looked like. It was a two-hour flight. I still couldn't get any rest. It was 15 February and I had just flown through my son's eleventh birthday. I wondered how they were doing. They, too, were on an adventure—dealing with no Dad being there. I had to change my thoughts or I would be an emotional dishrag when we landed.

The plane pulled up to the terminal in Adelaide, which was a beautiful, clean city positioned on the South Central Coast. It was an eight-hour drive to Woomera, where I would spend the next fifteen months. I was their new Chief of Tactical Operations. I would run the day-to-day operations of the site. I wondered if Chuck would be there. This was all strange to me. I had never been overseas before. I entered the terminal with my bag knowing I had to find Chuck and my luggage. Much of my personal belongings and household goods were already in transit by the Air Force and en route to Woomera. Suddenly, this guy waved and yelled out my name. It was him. It was pretty obvious, as he had a uniform on. Chuck was a major, and he came alone. We met and shook hands.

"Major, I am Chuck Gilmore. It's good to finally meet you. I know you're tired, it ain't an easy trip. Here, let me help you. We got a contract apartment near here in an Adelaide suburb called Glenelg, which will help get you caught up on the time changes. I think you will like it. And I have a couple of beers in the box that I know you will appreciate."

Hmm. I was already impressed. A nice enough guy, and had the sense to take care of the more important necessities. I was beginning to like this. But God, I was tired. I didn't remember ever being so tired.

I retrieved my belongings and we drove to a nearby apartment complex close to the beach. It wasn't far, just a couple of miles. It didn't take long. As we arrived I took note of the area. Wow! Glenelg was a beautiful spot on the beach. I could imagine my family and me vacationing in such a paradise.

It was late in the day, but I couldn't tell if it was because of my jet lag or if it was indeed late in the day. I think it was mid afternoon, but my head was in a fog. We entered the apartment and Chuck showed me around.

"We use this apartment a lot. We often have to come to Adelaide for one reason or another. It is open to anyone that has a reason to come down. Only business, of course. We have a couple of bedrooms, kitchen, den—you know, the usual stuff, but not much else." Chuck was quite businesslike and very thorough, but he had an air about him and a dry sense of humor. He joked a lot with little quips and I caught most of them, even though the jet lag prevented my full appreciation. We were to spend the night there and leave early in the morning for Woomera. God, it was hot in there, too. It had air-conditioning, but it was turned off. We found the switch and it soon became comfortable.

"Is it always this bloody hot down here?" I asked.

"Hell, this is our summer, and if you think this is hot, wait till you get to Woomera. Don't worry, your flat has AC." I think Chuck actually enjoyed my shock. "Hey, how about that beer I promised you?"

"Yeah, why not. Thanks. It's past happy hour time anyway." I sat down at the table and sort of just melted into the chair. He brought over some munchies and the beer. God, that tasted good, the brand didn't matter. "These Aussies sure know how to make a good beer," I said. I took a few swigs and noticed I was really getting tired, almost like I was drugged. I think the long trip was finally hitting me. As I was talking to Chuck and kibitzing about all the good things of life, I suddenly felt like someone was dragging a black curtain over me. It was disabling. It reminded me of that operation many years back when I flashed my classmate. This time I had my clothes on! The next time I was aware of anything, I found myself stretched out on a small cot and it was morning, or at least I thought it was. Little by little I started to remember where I was, and why. I was in Adelaide and on my way to somewhere in the Australian Outback!

"Hey, good morning. It's tomorrow. You were out. Did you sleep well? I did what I had to do watching you snore away the afternoon and evening. Thank God we hooked up TV here 'cause you would have been bloody boring. Did you sleep well?"

"Yes," I responded, still dazed at remembering what I had just experienced.

"You must have been seriously tired 'cause you collapsed facedown on the table. I picked your head up from the plate of cheese and crackers where you so aptly planted it, and I had to cart you over to the cot and let you rest. You were so unconscious. I am sure glad you are as skinny as you are. How do you feel?"

"Well, first of all, thanks for helping. It wasn't the beer, but it probably didn't help. I also am not used to sleeping in my clothes, but I appreciate your dragging me over there. So, what's the schedule?"

"I told the boss we would be on the way as soon as you were able to travel, so it's up to you."

"As much as I would like to check this town out, I suppose we should be on our way. I need a shower and a change of clothes, among other things, then we should go. I am hungry, but there doesn't seem to be much in the apartment. I think we need to get some food someplace."

"Yeah, go ahead and do what you have to do. You know where the bathroom is. And don't worry about food; I know a place just north of here on the road. I'll get most of the stuff in the car while you do your thing," he said. "You should be aware; it's a bit of a trek up there. Not much to look at. Lots of wide-open country, but it has its own personality. It usually takes about six or seven hours."

I took my shower, shaved, and was ready to go. I was actually quite anxious. I had never been there, or really anywhere, and this was a real experience. I sure missed my family, though. I had to figure out a way to get a phone call in. I mentioned my angst about family to Chuck.

"Hey, sure, where is my head? Of course, you need to call home. I should have been more on top of it. Sorry. Here, use this phone and call this number. We have an AUTOVON capability here and you can do what you have to do. I'll be in the other room. Good luck, sometimes the connection is a bit rough."

Chuck went into the other room while I dialed. I remember thinking, *God, please let them be there.* The phone rang, once, twice, and then a third time.

"Hello?" What a wonderful sound. It was my wife.

"Hi, honey. I made it to Adelaide. I love you. I miss you. How are the boys?"

"Oh, honey, it already seems like forever since we left you at the airport. Are you okay?"

"Oh, sweetheart, I already miss you and the boys so much. Yes, I'm fine. I am here with my sponsor, Major Chuck Gilmore, and we are about to go up the road to Woomera. It's a long drive from here. Are the boys nearby? I know it's late there."

"Yes, sweetheart, they're right here and anxious to talk to you."

They got on the phone and we talked about how proud I was of them to be strong while I was away. I asked how the birthday went. It was all good. No party, just a few friends and a cake, of course. They said they missed me but not to worry. They were on top of it. I acknowledged and told them how much I loved them. I had a brief return to my wife, we said our good-byes, and I promised to call as soon as I got to Woomera and was able. I didn't have a clue what the situation would be. It was late in Simi Valley and they were all tired, and apparently they had waiting until I called. I was glad I could. What an emotional tug—I wasn't prepared for it. I hung up the phone and called to Chuck for us to get going, and thanked him for letting me use the phone.

We tossed our things in the government car and pressed on. It was a bit strange for me to see everyone driving on the wrong side of the road. Of course, the car we had was Australian model and the wheel was on the correct side for them. I took a little while to meander through the streets and find the right road. It was a two-lane road called the Stuart Highway and would take us most of the way.

Adelaide was a beautiful town of about a million or so. The architecture looked a bit Victorian on a lot of the downtown buildings. The entire country's population was only about thirty million—a country roughly the size of the forty-eight U.S. states and filled to the brim with a population equivalent to that of California. Most everyone lived on the perimeter. Once you went about fifty clicks or kilometers inland you were in the true Outback.

Chuck was right. Once we were out of the city, we were really out there. Mostly flat reddish-brown plains, no trees to speak of, mainly bush with a few rolling hills. I was taking in all the sights and in my own world, thinking of how little it takes to change your life around. I had left a crowed city called Los Angeles a few hours ago, and now I found myself on the other side of the world and in the Southern Hemisphere on my way to a hot place. My calm was suddenly interrupted by Chuck.

"Just so you know, I checked out your flat yesterday and it appears ready for you. I suppose you will have to get some loaner cookware and stuff like that, but don't worry, we've all been through that. We want to get you settled as soon as we can. Oh, there's a barbie tonight at the DO's place. Starts around 1800 hours. You should plan on going to it. It will be a great opportunity to meet the people; besides, there's good food. I know they are anxious to meet you." We continued to get to know one another and exchanged thoughts about the idea of being in Australia.

"Yeah, I guess I'd like to go to the barbie, but I don't have any transport."

"Don't worry; we are all kinda like family there. I'll pick you up. Actually, it's not that far from your flat. If you knew Woomera you could easily walk it. But I'll come by."

Up ahead a ways out of town we found that café Chuck had referred to. It was nearly lunchtime and the hunger pains were creeping up. As soon as we entered, this guy came out from what I imagine was the kitchen.

"G'day mates! What do ya have?" I could tell this place was truly in the back country and there were likely no others nearby. This might be the last chance to get something to eat, so I looked at menu and ordered what sounded simple enough.

"I'll have the hamburger and chips," I said.

"Ah! You're bloody Yanks, hey?" He grinned broadly from ear to ear. "No worries, mates, she'll be right. I'll have it for ya straightaway."

We were guilty. We were Yanks, and once we opened our mouths and uttered a word the secret was disclosed. Foreigners in a strange land. Me especially!

In addition to the cook there was a waitress, and she served our order. I looked at it and was surprised by its size. Lo and behold, the damned thing looked about four inches high, and the burger was topped with a couple of bacon slices and a fried egg! Fries were called chips; I knew that much, but I didn't expect both breakfast and lunch in one sitting, and stuck between two bun halves.

Chuck noticed my shock. "They always make 'em that way down here. If you want something different you have to ask. They like to eat." He smiled as if he had expected the whole thing.

When I asked the lady for some ketchup for the chips, she looked at me like I was some alien or something. Chuck mentioned discreetly that they called it sauce. They also expected that you wanted vinegar for your chips and it was there on the table. I tried it. Hmm, not bad. Well, my first learning experience in the land down under went off smoothly. It tasted great.

I was ready to proceed. Stepping back outside was a true temperature shock. It must have been 110 degrees at least. Thank God for AC.

We finally made it to Woomera. The road that we became so intimate with in the last several hours was mostly straight and boring. I learned it had been only a couple of years back that the road had its first covering of pavement. It was a dirt road, as were many of the roads this far into the Outback. It was a flat land. All around the ground was almost red. I imagined it was like Mars, only with an atmosphere humans could deal with. It was hot, too, with the temperature exceeding 110 degrees. Chuck had said that it would be hotter than Adelaide, and he was right!

God, who would want to be here? I thought. This was a little town of about two thousand inhabitants; mostly Aussie, of course, but the Americans made up about six hundred. The name of the town came from the aboriginal term meaning "throwing stick," a device used for hunting. I later found out that many of the current residents actually grew up there and hadn't ventured much farther than the limits of the perimeter road. I couldn't imagine that. I remembered growing up in a very small town, too, but under extremely different circumstances; as poor as we were, it was high class compared to this place.

The town had many past lives—all military missions with mostly domestic and European countries. They even dabbled a bit with nuclear testing in the far distance of the Outback; not in Woomera, but it was their headquarters and center of operations. Now it was the living quarters for essential personnel assigned to work a joint classified mission with the United States and Australia. The place had a gate just outside of the main entrance. but it wasn't manned anymore as it had been in Woomera's heyday. It was opened up a couple of years prior to my being there.

There were two gas stations. Fuel was expensive, too, and sold by the liter. In the center of the town was a small shopping area. A little grocery store, an ice cream bar, and a shop that sold most of what one normally needs in the way of over-the-counter drugs, newspapers, writing materials, cards, etc. Across the street from there was a theater, and next to it was the swimming pool. Not bad for being so far away from real civilization. The town received water from the Murray River, which was more that two hundred kilometers south. It was delivered via a two-foot-diameter pipeline. Water was a very valuable item that far inland. The town had a police station, too, but only two cops. It was there we had to go to get an Australian driver's license, but that would be later. There were lots of empty houses which were built to support the larger population of around six thousand in the more active times.

After a short driving tour of the town we arrived at my flat on Wirruna Street, which intersected with the perimeter road and was across from the entrance gate. They called it the NASA quarters. It was built to support NASA during the Mercury, Gemini, and Apollo days. NASA had a tracking station just outside of Woomera and near the one where I would be working. *The American movie* The Right Stuff *features a scene of the Woomera Ground Station.* The buildings were brick structures holding eight apartments or flats— four above and four below. They were all the same. Mine was the corner flat on the first floor. The main room windows looked directly at the guard gate. It was a nice place. There were two bedrooms, a large living room, a full kitchen, a bath and shower, and plenty of storage room. Air-conditioning was there, but with window units. Nicer than I had imagined. I only had my bags that I flew with, but that was enough to sort of get settled with.

Chuck left, promising he would be by to pick me up for the barbie in a couple of hours. I had just enough time to get the belongings I came with into the place, explore a bit, and take another shower. God, it was hot, and I was a smelly mess. I gazed out the living room windows and looked across the road at the entry gate. I stared for a moment at that gate and whispered to myself, "I came in that gate and in fifteen months I will go out that gate." Fifteen months, what a long time that seemed. I needed to nap; jet lag for that distance takes a couple of days—or so they told me. I had no idea what the barbie was going to be like, but felt I had to go. What the hell else did I have on my agenda?

I stirred from a half nap, hearing a knock on the door; sure enough, it was Chuck.

"Are ya ready? Take your time. This is not a command performance."

"Yeah, come in. I was just napping a bit. I'm still getting this jet lag thing squared away."

"I know what you're talking about. It usually takes a day or two. No worries, nothing here is that formal, we have time."

"Chuck, you said the barbie is at the DO's house. His name is Bart Smith, right?"

"Yeah, that's right."

"You know, that name is real familiar to me for some reason." I didn't know why, but I would soon find out.

"He's okay, all businesslike. Takes his job very seriously. But what else would you expect. I think you will like him. He sure is anxious to get you here. He was really disappointed that you didn't want to bring your family, though. I imagine he'll bring that item up with you tonight, so heads up."

"Yeah, thanks. Well, when we spoke on the phone, I told you the reasons I chose not to bring them while I was still working the MSE program. I can't do that to them. Besides, I have a by-name job offer back in the world of the Secretary of the Air Force, Special Projects. Remember, I told you they were holding that position open for me for the fifteen months I am here, but if my family came with me I would be forced to stay here for twenty-four months. Anyway, we talked about that. I will not change my decision. I'm ready if you are."

"Yup, let's go. It ain't that far. I should remind you that typically you are to bring something to pass at a barbie. It's an Aussie custom. Since you're new, you are not to worry about that. But for the future, they do sell barbie packs at the store."

We drove a little way and found the DO's house. A nice enough house with a small yard that even had a little patch of green grass. It was one of the original houses built years before when there was a larger population. Apparently everyone was in the backyard. There were lots of voices and laughter. We went around back. Chuck started to introduce me. It was a mixed crowd; male, female, civilians, Aussies, etc. In the distance, near the corner of the yard, was a little campfire built between a couple of cinder blocks. It had a thick metal plate on top of the blocks. One of the Aussie guys seemed to be in charge of that part.

"Ah, there you are. Welcome to Woomera. I'm Colonel Bart Smith. How was the trip?"

"Thanks, the trip was good. I'm still in a bit of jet lag, but I'll be okay." *Hmm,* I thought, *he introduced himself as "Colonel" Bart Smith.* I thought he was a lieutenant colonel. He was! I kept looking at him, thinking that it wasn't just the name I had heard before, he looked familiar, too. "Bart, I have to ask, have we met before? You look familiar." Knowing he was a lieutenant colonel and I had a line number for the same rank I felt comfortable calling him by his first name.

"Well, yeah, you do, too. Years ago I was in Titan II at McConnell. Was that it? I was on crew there."

"Me, too! From 1970 to 1974." *Wow, what a coincidence,* I thought. This would be great, having a boss who shared a common assignment from years past. There it was, 1985, and of all places to run into a fellow missileer. I was feeling better about this assignment. That feeling wouldn't last long, however.

"Yeah, I was there a little ahead of you. I think I remember you now. I was in the 533rd SMS. You were, too, right?"

"Yes, I think we were both lieutenants then. I was a second lieutenant, I think, when I first saw you. You were a lieutenant, too, if I am not mistaken."

"First lieutenant!"

"Oh, well, a lieutenant is a lieutenant. We were both young."

"What the hell are you saying? There is a goddamned big difference. I outranked you. I outranked you then and I still outrank you. I know you have a line number for lieutenant colonel. I pinned on a year ago."

Well, my balloon just popped. Boy, did that hit a nerve. It's like a switch was flipped from the reasonable and congenial Dr. Jekyll to the monster Mr. Hyde. The guy I thought I could be friends with was not the guy I thought he might be. Now I was remembering him more and more. I remembered he had a nickname back at McConnell—"Black Bart." What an ass! What a legacy. I had fifteen months to go and he was my boss, so I had no choice but to button up and deal with it.

"You're right, SIR!" I couldn't restrain my louder military voice. But I held back my growing contempt. In my entire life I could never hide my emotions; they were always displayed on my face like a neon sign. This was one of those situations. My face must have broadcast "what an ass" from ear to ear.

I had my first encounter with my immediate boss and it wasn't good—and it was at his home in the dunga (Aboriginal name for desert) of Australia. I thought it best to continue to humor him by making comments that inflated his ego. I wanted to avert a confrontation. I got a beer and mingled, introducing myself as I went. He was the only schmuck in the entire evening; all of his guests were very nice and welcomed me. I wanted a fresh start with Bart and looked for an opportunity, and it came.

Later, I decided to approach Bart again to try to explain my personal situation. I thought maybe I should wait until we met more formally, but decided in favor of discussing it with him right then. After all, he had had a couple of beers and was again in a mood that seemed approachable.

"Bart, I need to tell you about a personal situation at home. My father is dying of cancer. I don't know how long he has but he won't last fifteen months. I will likely need to go home on emergency leave at some point. I just wanted to give you a heads-up."

Bart didn't say anything. Not even that he was sorry about my dad. Then, out of the blue, he pulled me by the arm a bit to the right and pointed over the crowd to a woman standing near the fence.

"Do you see that girl over there? She just lost her mom. She didn't go home. She bore up and stayed here where she was needed." He continued pointing, but in a different direction. "Do you see that guy in the checkered shirt with the beer? He's that woman's husband who just lost his dad. He stayed, too. No emergency leave. So, Major, I think you should think about those two before you ask me for emergency leave. What we do here is important and we need all hands on station at all times—doing their job."

I was so pissed I couldn't think of anything to say at first. "Are you telling me that I am not authorized emergency leave? If you are, we have a huge problem, and it is only my first day here." I was about to ask to contact the inspector general. That might be my only recourse. He had no right to deny me emergency leave. We were not in a combat zone.

He didn't respond. He just looked at me, perhaps thinking he had miscalculated in his assessment of me. I was not going to take any shit from him. Thinking of this, I knew I could have easily kissed his ass and it would have been all better, but I don't kiss ass. Never have, never will. We left each other's company. I tried to forget the conversation and move about. I imagined he felt that he had a bull on his hands—and he did. He touched hallowed ground when it came to my family, and especially my dad's situation, and he knew it.

"We'll talk tomorrow," he said, and then walked away. I kept glancing over at him, and from time to time he would look over at me as well. *I think he got the point*, I thought.

I sampled the food and had another beer or two. I was ready to get back to the flat and do some more unpacking—maybe write a letter. I needed to figure out how I was going to get by on this assignment while working with a first-class asshole. God! I was truly pissed. Tomorrow was going to be hell.

I didn't have a car yet so I had to take the common bus which stopped just outside my flat. It was a full bus, but it took no time to travel the fourteen kilometers to the site. It was my first day on the job and I had already had a bad experience the night before with the boss. During the ride I was preparing myself for an encore. I wasn't a happy camper. The others on the bus kept looking at me as if I were some strange alien. Nope, just the new guy, and for many of them, their boss.

I did the expected thing and reported to the commander, Colonel Miller. What a stark difference from his DO, Black Bart, who sat in the adjoining office. The colonel and I had a nice talk. He gave me assurances that whatever I needed to get settled, just ask. He said he was very happy I had arrived and wished me the best on this assignment. He also understood about my father and would make available to me the AUTOVON network to call home any time I needed to check in on him. He wanted me to be as comfortable with my situation as he could make it. I thanked him and had started to leave, when I saw Black Bart coming down the hall. *Okay, here we go*, I thought, wondering if I had just experienced the "good cop/bad cop" scenario. I hoped not. I liked the commander.

"Ah, you found the place," he said. "Come on in, let's get a fresh start. We have the usual stuff to discuss with anyone new." I wondered if he was bipolar because this was not the ass that I met last night. Or was he?

"Yes, sir, I took the bus. I will have to somehow get my own transportation. Perhaps you know someone who wants to sell." I was trying to think of ways to converse and seem like I, too, didn't want to recall the encounter at the barbie.

"Sit down, Major. Yeah, I think there is an Aussie woman over at Woomera West—that's our personnel and staff area—leaving to join her husband in Adelaide. He used to work here but left for a new job. Her name is Mary; she works in the housing office. In fact, you'll meet her when you process in. That's your first action: finish processing in. What I want to do today is take you on a short tour of the station and let you get the lay of the land. Your job as Chief of Tactical Operations is key here. We can't screw it up. I think you know where I am coming from. This is serious business here and everything we do is an international event." Hmm, not once had he mentioned my potential need for emergency leave. "Why can't we convince you to bring your family? You know there is still time. I don't like short-timers." *Ah*, I thought, *here it comes.*

"Thanks for the contact about a car. I'll check into it. As for my family, I am sorry, Bart, but I explained all that to you and others when you called me in LA. I have a job waiting for me when I return. I can't discuss it because of its classified nature. So, I am afraid that I will be a short-timer, but believe me, I won't let you down." I took the chance at calling him Bart. He didn't seem to mind, but he never called me by my first name, only my last name or by my rank. Oh, well.

"I hope not. You have to realize that this mission is extremely important. We need people like you who know operations."

"I understand, and as long as I am working here you have that expertise of mine in full force to the best of my abilities. But the place I came from needs operationally experienced people, too."

"Bullshit, that place you came from is hardly Air Force. It's the Hollywood Air Force made up by a bunch of eggheads with no concept of reality."

Now he got me pissed again. I took a breath and then said, "Bart, where the hell do you think the satellite you are so proud of came from, anyway? I know how and where it came from, that Hollywood Air Force. I know the history of its development. I know the technical details of this satellite and its name before it got the name you know it by. Bart, you must realize it was due to the efforts of those eggheads that create tools like your beloved satellite that helps keep our country free. If they didn't do their job and do it well, you wouldn't have one. Let me add, I happen to be one of those eggheads that also just happens to have half a career in missile operations. They think what I have to offer is also important. It's final, Bart. Sorry. I will stay with my fifteen-month tour. I have to make my own career decisions whenever I can do so and I did—just as you did, Bart."

"Oh, I know where you're coming from, but if you change your mind I can guarantee you a four-star endorsement on your next OER."

That was his idea of a threat. I had had many general officer endorsements and been in the limelight for enhancing my promotion potential. By saying what he said, he was telling me that he would do anything to screw me on my next efficiency report if I didn't go along with him on moving my family there. No matter, I already had a line number for lieutenant colonel and that would be enough, if necessary.

"Thanks, but I am firm on my decision, Bart. I'll say it again, I won't let you down."

"Okay, let's go on a short tour here, and then you can take one of the staff cars and go get yourself in-processed."

I took the tour with him. It went well. No slams, no reference to my being a short-timer, etc. I was again thinking that my hard stand on the issue of my family and my next assignment might have changed his view of me. I had to hope. We had to get along. Over the years I had learned how to cope with any adversary and I think I held up well. If my encounter with Black Bart had happened years earlier in my career, the outcome might have been different.

I took the car and went to Woomera West. I found the housing office and entered.

"Excuse me, I am looking for Mary," I said, then introduced myself and asked the person if she knew where I could find her.

"That would be me, Major. G'day to you. What can I help you with?"

"Well, I have to be here anyway for in-processing, but was told by Black—uh, I mean, Bart Smith—that you might be interested in selling a car. I'll be in need of some type of transport fairly quickly."

"Yes, I am moving with my husband to Adelaide and I need to sell the damned thing. I don't have a lot of time, he is already settled there and I need to close up here and get on with it. It ain't much, but it gets me where I need to go in the village. You can have a look at it if you like," she said.

I did and I liked it. It was a 1966 Volkswagen, not the greatest in the world, but it ran—well, most of the time. She wanted $750.00A; the price was right so we made a deal. I could come by anytime to get it. It took a day or two but that was all.

The boss gave me a couple of days to get myself settled. I eventually found my place at the site. I was getting comfortable in my position, although I continued to be very cautious around ole Black Bart. I had personal responsibility for just under fifty crew personnel, half of them Aussie. The crews were made up of six persons; two officers and four enlisted. The job was classified and still is.

It was a lonely existence but I kept busy. I had to keep myself from getting too close to anyone due to my position. I was the third-ranking officer in the entire town and often had to make decisions which required absolute impartiality. The place was teeming with the undercurrent of rumors. Idle hands find things to do. I renamed the town Rumora as opposed to Woomera. One day that bit of small-town personality became personal with me. I was in front of my flat shaking out a rug when the lady from upstairs noticed and came out and leaned over the rail.

"Hi, how are you doing? Getting settled?" she asked. Her name was Kate. She was in Woomera just visiting her husband for few months and would return to the States soon.

"Oh, hi, Kate. Yeah, I'm pretty well settled now. Just doing a bit of cleaning. This red powder we call dunga dust sure does get everywhere," I said.

"I know what you mean. I won't miss it when I finally get to go home. Oh, by the way, you must know that the word is out about you."

"What word? What are you talking about?" I sensed she was teasing, but wasn't sure. She had this half smirk on her mug.

"Well, er, um—your affair."

"My affair? What affair? What the hell are you talking about?"

"Mary's car seems to be parked in front of your flat a lot lately. Rumors are all over the village that she is shacking up with you. They all know that her husband is gone."

I was shocked. They warned me about this place before I left to come over. I was getting hit with my first rumor encounter.

"No kidding. Well, tell me, Kate, am I having fun? Because it ain't worth the gamble if I'm not having some real fun."

"Well, you look like you're okay. Hell, I am just kidding, I know the facts, but I thought you'd appreciate it. I actually heard two women talking over at the store. You were the hot topic. I wouldn't worry too much about it, though."

"Hell, this place is incredible. I heard about it before I came here, Kate, but I never thought much of it. Even if I wanted to have an affair, which I don't, I wouldn't."

I let that rumor pass with a smile, but with a refreshed view of how dangerous this little place in the middle of nowhere could be. I would henceforth be ultra careful to keep the rumormongers at bay.

Time passed slowly in the dunga. Not a whole lot to do. You had to invent ways to occupy your free time. I wrote tons of letters to my wife and sons. I took a lot of walks and attended many of the cricket and footy games on Saturday mornings.

It was a Saturday morning. The sun was beaming as usual. The footy game was just starting. It was at one of the town ovals. Nearby the oval was a pub. There were four pubs in the town. The Aussies take great pride in their games and their pubs. They love a challenge and boast about their beer. I found a place to sit next to some friends I had made. Nice people. Not everyone was a rumormonger. This game of footy was one of the things the Aussies pride themselves on. It was like American football, but without the protective padding.

"Hi, Carla, how's it going?" Carla was the wife of one of the Aussie crew members that worked for me.

"Hiya, Major," she replied.

"Which team are you rooting for, Carla?" I asked.

She looked at me as if I had committed some carnal sin. She gulped a bit of her beer and then offered up a response.

"Well, Major, I think you need to understand that we don't 'root' for our teams. The correct word is barrack."

"Barrack, eh? Hmm, I never heard that word before. What's wrong with 'rooting'?" I asked.

"Let's see, how do I explain this? Rooting is what animals do, Major, it's a sexual thing. Barracking is what we do to cheer on our teams."

"Oh my God, sorry about that." I had learned a new word. And all this time I thought Aussies spoke English.

I continued to watch the game and sucked down a beer or two. It was getting hot and that Victoria Bitter sure tasted good.

"Oh my God, look at that guy, he's pretty wild. If he doesn't watch it he'll be on his fanny."

As soon as I said that she did it again. I looked at her. She had this terribly uncomfortable painful look on her face. I got a nudge from one of the blokes sitting next to me on the other side. He was holding back a laugh.

"What's the matter?" I asked.

"Well, Major, I don't know how to tell you this, but…" Carla was unsure of just how to inform me of another sin against the Aussie language. Again she hesitated.

"But what?" I asked. Just then, the team made the play, and as they did my forecast of the action came true. "See that? That bloke fell flat on his fanny—hard, too. I bet that hurt."

Carla couldn't hold back anymore. "You see," she said hesitantly, "he doesn't have a 'fanny.' Women have 'em but you blokes don't. Do you get my drift?"

"Ah, okay. God, I am screwed up. Thanks for the help. Perhaps I should just keep my mouth shut."

"No, ya don't have to do that, we understand you Yanks." The guy on the other side broke out in open laughter and jabbed me in the ribs.

"Why the hell didn't you say something?" I asked him. He knew all along.

So that little lesson in Aussie English came shortly after I arrived. It didn't take much to get into trouble in the midst of the dunga.

I worked long hours to pass the time. I had to keep myself as busy as I could to make the time pass faster. I continued to call my wife and boys as often as possible. The time difference made my calls a real challenge. I also kept checking with Dad. It wasn't going to be long. I went on day by day, thinking that the Red Cross would soon be contacting my unit for emergency orders to return home. The policy was that the caring doctor had to notify the Red Cross and then they coordinated with the Air Force. Why the Red Cross had to be in the middle of it was beyond me, but it was.

Good ole Black Bart and I had made our peace for the sake of professionalism. I was in good company about him and I knew it. Even the Aussies didn't like him. I wondered whether his wife did. One day a true miracle happened. I arrived at the site was getting on with my day when one of the other staff persons came up to me in the hallway.

"Hey, did you hear that Smith has orders?"

An uncontrollable grin suddenly appeared on my face. "No, when is he leaving?"

"Within the month, I'm not sure."

"God, that is great news," I said. Just thinking of that made the rest of day and those next few weeks a lot lighter. I couldn't wait. His replacement was due in any day.

Time passed and Smith departed for the States— thank God! His replacement was a vast improvement. A nice guy. Then the inevitable happened.

The phone rang early in the morning. It was my wife. Dad was getting worse and there was no hope. I needed to come home as soon as possible. She said the doctor had already called the Red Cross and I should be hearing soon. I told her how much I loved her and the boys. So there I was, stranded on this island called Australia and my father was fading fast. I prayed.

I called the boss and told him about the call from my wife. He said that he would check with personnel to see if emergency orders were in the works, but reminded me they needed an official notification from the Red Cross. I told him they were working it on the other end. He told me to relax and it would all be fine. It was. About an hour later I was notified that I could pick up my orders and was free to travel whenever I could get it coordinated. They helped me a lot. I was in a fog but it all worked out. My orders were in hand and the tickets were purchased. I was on my way. I had thirty days before I had to come back.

One of my friends volunteered to drive me to Adelaide. We left around six in the morning the day after I had my orders. We were on the way. I was sitting in the front seat and John was driving. His wife, Lynn, was sitting in the backseat. The sun was just barely above the horizon and it was already becoming a typical hot South Australia day.

We were all tired and no one was talking. The radio was on but not very loud. There wasn't much to listen to in the Outback. All the stations were very distant. I leaned back in the seat in a daze, thinking of the trip ahead. I was wondering how Mom was doing with all she had to deal with. I wondered about our boys. I hoped they would understand. I thought about the pain Dad must be in and prayed that his release would soon be there. The ride to Adelaide was not an easy one and I really appreciated John and Lynn taking the time and effort to do it for me. I had real friends. They knew I realized that.

I was just sitting there in a bit of a trance when I heard a voice. But I couldn't, no one was speaking. It sounded like my dad.

"Son, I told you I'd come. I am here in Australia with you."

I was in shock. I sat up and looked at John, then turned and looked at Lynn. Everything seemed normal. John was looking ahead at the road and driving the car. Lynn was reading.

"Did you guys say something?" I asked.

"Say something? No, why?" John asked.

"Oh, nothing. I thought I heard a voice."

"Well, the radio is on, but it is more noise than anything, I didn't say anything and neither did Lynn. Are you okay?"

"Yeah, I'm okay." I noted the time as 0730 hours and settled back in the seat. My mind was confused. I had heard him. I really had heard him. It was Dad. He had told me that he would be in Australia before I returned. I remembered telling him to keep up that attitude.

We arrived at the Adelaide airport on schedule and I was soon on my way. It was going to be a flight doglegging through Honolulu. I was anxious to get home. I had coordinated my schedule with my wonderful wife and she promised to be at LAX to meet me. She did.

What a beautiful sight. There she was. I was just about to exit the ramp into the terminal when I noticed her face. She was sad and shaking her head as if to say no. I nodded at her. I mouthed the words, "I know."

We embraced, and after a long hug and kisses we went to the baggage claim. As we were walking, we talked and I caught up on the latest.

"What time did he die?" I asked her. "Wait, don't tell me. I bet it was around eleven or twelve on the fifteenth, right?"

"How did you know? You had no way of knowing."

"Honey, I have to tell you something, but it sounds really strange. Do you remember when I told you what Dad told me last February, when we visited him before I left for Australia? He said that he'd be there in Australia before I came home. I told him that was a great attitude, thinking he was just trying to stay positive for me."

"Yeah, I remember. So?"

"Well, as we were traveling to the airport I heard Dad. He said he was there with me. I was stunned. No one was talking, and I know my dad's voice. It was him. I also checked the clock and noted the time. It corresponds to his time of death."

She looked at me without saying anything. I was tearing up. We were in the airport in the midst of hundreds of strangers and I was standing there waiting for my bags, crying, with my wife holding me. We retrieved my bags and departed for home. What a complicated set of emotions. I wanted to be home and Dad got me there. I was anxious to see the boys. Two hours later we were with them. We hugged and hugged. God, I loved my little family.

We talked a lot about Grandpa and the plans for the service. I was to read a poem he had written two years ago. It was called "Grieve Not For Me." He wrote it soon after he was pronounced terminal. There was no hope, but he had some, enough to know there was another place—a better place. He wanted us to know. I read the poem. It was a beautiful service. Yes, Dad was there, too.

I'll never forget that day. It was all true; Dad came to visit me in Australia. I don't know how but I know it happened. He was there. He kept his word. Just as he always did. I'd give anything to hear him call me Bub one more time like he did so many years ago. I loved him so.

TEN

More challenges
Transitions in the works

A few days after the memorial service for Dad I returned to my duties in Woomera. Once again I was going to leave my family, once again promising to return as soon as I could and that I would write and call often. The boys had just lost their grandpa and now they were going to lose their dad, too. I had another six months to go. My heart ached for them.

My wife was able to make a trip to come over and see me for a few weeks, but unfortunately with school the boys had to stay with friends. While she was there, my unit promoted me to lieutenant colonel ahead of time. Where was Black Bart? That process typically wasn't done and takes a high level of approval. Needless to say, I was honored, and so was my beautiful wife.

I felt the pain in my wallet, though. It was customary to throw some sort of party for promotions. Well, we did just that. The town had a small park, and once the pin-on ceremony was completed I had arranged to buy beer for whoever wanted to come. What a deal that was. I believe the entire town was there—several hundred, for sure. They all liked their beer. I didn't care; it was a phenomenal experience.

The entire town responded to my wife being there with me for that short while. They treated her like a queen. She blended in beautifully. Our only problem was missing our sons. Too soon it was time for her to go. I had to stay another five months, but it was good to have her there for a little while.

On that fateful day of 28 January 1986, we were in Adelaide getting ready to go to the airport. I was in the shower. My wife began pounding on the bathroom door.

"Honey! You've got to get out here, now!" She was frantic.

"What's the matter?"

"I don't know, it's on the TV, something is wrong with the shuttle. They keep talking about the teacher."

I noticed the fright in her eyes and stared at the TV.

"Oh my God! The shuttle just blew up," I said.

I also knew who the crew was. Although the news reporters kept talking about the loss of the teacher, the entire crew of seven had just perished. I could see from the news clip it must have been the solid rocket motors. I, of course, didn't really know, and neither did NASA. On board were three very good friends of mine: Dick Scobee, Ellison (El) Onizuka, and Judy Resnik. I didn't know the others. I felt like someone had kicked me hard in the belly. Tears began to well up in my eyes and roll down my face. My wife came over and just held me. "Oh my God!" was all I could say.

It was STS 51L, and as the news unfolded I learned that I was correct in observing the hot gases spewing from one of the solid joints. It acted like a cutting torch, blowing hot, deadly gas into the main propellant tank. Once that happened the crew was doomed. There was no way. The shuttle broke up, but the crew compartment remained intact until it collided with the ocean some fifty thousand feet below. I flashed back to that late night at the Cape, when Crippen and I had a talk and I asked him about those solid motors. His reply was that they were probably the safest part of the entire vehicle. What haunting words!

What a sad day it was. I was taking my wife to the airport and wasn't going to see her for another five months, and I had witnessed the destruction of the shuttle.

"Oh, hon. I used to harass El about sucking up to George Abbey for another mission. I feel so shitty about that. Dick Scobee and I worked the launch and landing protocol for the first shuttle mission. He flew the chase plane. Judy, well, she was beautiful in all ways. A wonderful woman, humble, and very smart."

"I'm so sorry, hon," was all she could say. It hit her hard, too.

"Those poor people and their families." I felt the loss deeply.

Eventually we got ourselves together and headed for the airport. It was a quiet drive. Soon she was gone. I felt emptiness deep inside that hurt so bad. Now I had to get back on the road to return to Woomera alone. My mind was in a fog. My wife was on her way home to the boys and I was headed for this godforsaken piece of Australian desert—all because it was my job.

I walked in my flat. It felt like she should still be there. She wasn't. I went into the kitchen area. There on the table sat her coffee cup. I could see the lipstick on its rim. I nearly cried. I had to get out of there. I took a long walk, alone. I had a lot on my mind, but I had to find myself. I had to get through this.

May 1986

The plane had just landed at LAX. There to meet me were my lovely wife and our beautiful sons. God, thank God, I was home to stay. What a wonderful feeling. We talked, we sang, we laughed. The ride home seemed shorter for some reason. Perhaps it was the boys that helped me pass the time.

We were on the 118 freeway and near the off-ramp to our housing development. The house was visible from the highway. I searched to see if I could find it. Lo and behold, there it was. Something was different. There was a massive tarp covering most of the front of the garage. On it were the words: "Welcome home Dad—we love you." The entire neighborhood could see this. I felt so loved. Tears were in my eyes. God, it felt good to be home.

I made the necessary adjustments. So did my wife. She didn't have to make all the decisions anymore. The boys took a little time getting used to having me around and my wife helped by including me. Soon we were all back to normal. We were again a family—together and happy.

ELEVEN

New horizons of duty
And then let free

Once I was settled at home from my overseas tour and after a short break, I had to check in with my new duty station.

I was assigned to the National Reconnaissance Office. The name at the time was classified, but in later years the existence of this office was declassified. However, the internal workings remain classified. I can say, however, that our job was to create, launch, and manage the special space assets for overhead surveillance. This was the outfit of eggheads Black Bart Smith so affectionately alluded to. For the most part, my job in this outfit was and remains classified to this day. Suffice it to say that what I did and the people I worked with made me extremely proud to be an American.

I retired from the Air Force effective 31 October 1989. I was and am a truly blessed Air Force officer. My retirement ceremony was attended by my family, one sister, my uncle from England, and of course my mother; missing but present was Dad. The retiring official, Major General Nathan Lindsay, gave me one hell of a nice sendoff. He spoke directly to my family when he said that I reflected the best of what it means to be an officer. That my most valued asset was that of integrity. When he spoke those words I thought of Dad, because he was the same kind of guy.

I moved as gracefully as I could into civilian life with various jobs. I eventually ended up coming back to Vandenberg for a job I thought would last the rest of my working life. It didn't. After three years on the job as a Payload Systems Engineer, I was notified by management that a massive cutback was going to occur. I had a couple of months to find a new job before this one was done. I compiled a long list of contacts and started to work my network. Suddenly, one day I thought of my old friend Bob Crippen.

"Hello, office of the center director, may I help you?" The voice on the line was Crip's secretary. Crippen had retired from active astronaut duty and had been promoted to director of Kennedy Space Center, Florida.

I introduced myself, and asked if the director was in and if he could find time to speak with me. "Just a minute, sir, I'll see if he can." It wasn't long before I heard a familiar voice on the other end.

"Hey, boy, it has been a long time. How are you?" Crip hadn't changed. He was the same friendly guy as ever.

I explained what I had been doing, that I had retired and was now in Vandenberg but was on a layoff list, as were hundreds of others.

"Oh, I know you had retired and were at Vandenberg. Been keeping track of the team, so to speak. What can I do to help?"

"Well, I wanted to get your permission put your name as a reference on my resume. I thought it wouldn't hurt, but I wouldn't do it without your permission. I realize your position and all, Crip."

"Heck, sure you can," he said. He gave me his personal office fax number and a special number so I wouldn't have to go through hell to get to him, should I need to. "You know, as long as there is an Al Gore in office, there will be an EOS space program. We need someone with your talents at Vandenberg to help some of us NASA weenies. Let me see what I can do."

"Hey, thanks, Crip. I really appreciate it."

When we hung up I felt so relieved. I needed a job and I didn't want to move. My company would have kept me on without a layoff, but that meant moving to Denver, which I wasn't going to do.

Two weeks later, my office phone rang.

"Hello," I answered. I stated my name and asked if I could help.

"Well, yes. You don't know me. My name is Don Miller and I work for NASA at the Goddard Spaceflight Center in Maryland. I was given your name by one of our senior directors, Mr. Vern Weyres. I understand you might be looking for a job."

I was taken totally by surprise. I then recalled my conversation with Crip and wondered if this was because of him working something behind the scenes. "Er, yes, I am looking for another position. I have been told that due to the budget shortfalls our company will lay off about a third of the people, and unfortunately I am on the list." I explained about the possible Denver assignment, but stressed that I was looking to stay at Vandenberg.

"I see. Well, do you think we can get together today sometime to meet face-to-face? I think I may have an opportunity for you."

"Yes, sir. Where do you want to meet?" I said anxiously.

"I am at the NASA resident office here on the base, Building 840. Do you think you could meet here in, say, an hour?"

"Absolutely. See you soon."

He gave me details of exactly where Building 840 was and which room he'd be in. I was so eager. I hoped I truly had what he was looking for. I phoned Crip back, explained what I had just experienced, and expressed my gratitude.

"Crip, I don't know what you did and I don't want to, but thanks."

"Hey, we can't afford to lose good people. I hope it works out for you. Vern Weyres is a good man. I am sure he'll treat you fine."

I interviewed, and in a short time I was moving from the North Base to the South Base, Building 840. My job was to be the government contractual representative for Goddard for the medium and small expendable booster rocket programs. I loved it. And I didn't have to move.

I dove into all aspects of the job. Delta, Atlas, Pegasus, Scout, Titan—all examples of what I was responsible to oversee. I learned a lot. And I excelled.

This was just another example of how my life continues to be centered on space and space-related activities. I have been truly blessed. I am now retired from active employment. The sum of my emotions is vast and runs deep. I have touched many areas that most only dream of. I have witnessed great tragedy, and been conditioned with challenges. There are others with a greater story to tell, and they should, but I feel fortunate to be able to tell this one.

I continue to think of that day so many years ago. Many would say that one cannot recall things in so much detail from a time when one was so young. I, however, can. Two ladies approached my sandbox, knelt down and touched my face, and gave me the message that my future was going to be bright and secure. Indeed, my life was secure. I am a happy man. But who were those ladies?

EPILOGUE

All my life I was challenged by dealing with a ghost-like being of someone I didn't know. It was that challenge, however, that ultimately gave me the guts to bear up and go forward. I was adopted in 1954 by a man who gave his all for a ready-made family he accepted as his own blood. I was given his name, but the original one was and still is a part of me. The dad that sired me was a dropout dad. He had his problems. We were better off that he was not around. But that didn't erase the problem I had as a youngster in trying to live down the name. I was not a junior, but I nevertheless had his first and last name. As the years passed, I had a growing desire to find out more about the family of which I was a part, but didn't want to do so and hurt the man that gave me everything—my dad. The man that at first called me Bub, but later called me son.

I became more interested in my heritage. I knew I was of German descent and inexplicably proud of it. My great-great-grandfather came from Germany in 1846. I began learning more about this German connection. My interest in that country so far away grew stronger as the years went by. I also had the urge to learn the language and through self-study I did.

It was the late summer of 2004. My wife and I decided to take a trip to Germany. There were no specific plans. We just wanted to be tourists. We were on the autobahn traveling south from Berlin. The radio was playing. It was a beautiful day. I thought of how this country could be so beautiful with such a destructive past. Few signs of the devastation of the great wars were apparent. Suddenly, I felt a pang. An odd feeling came over me. A déjà vu.

"Honey, this is strange. I feel like I've been here before." It was a mix of new emotions that I could not explain. A bit of homesickness combined with the exhilaration of being in such a beautiful country. The feeling was real and strong.

"What are you talking about?" my wife responded.

"I don't know. I just have the feeling of being home. I can't explain it."

We dropped the subject and enjoyed the rest of our vacation.

Many months later, I was at the computer and typed in my original last name just for the fun of it. I got a hit. It was from a man named Jason. Apparently, he was looking for the lineage of his family. We discovered we were related. I gave him my phone number. He called. He had done his homework. He forwarded me information on several people in Germany possessing the same last name as mine before adoption.

My interest surged. I decided to compose a short letter in German and send it to each of them, introducing myself and asking if they knew of any American relatives. I got lucky. One day, a few weeks later, I received a letter from an individual in Germany providing me with a woman's name, Nancy. She lives in Fairchild, Wisconsin, only twenty miles from where I grew up. I found her phone number and called.

She is a cousin of mine that I never knew. Our great-grandfathers were brothers and the sons of the man who emigrated from Bacharach, Germany. We exchanged a lot of information. She sent me a package of documentation on the family tree.

In the summer of 2007, my wife and I traveled back to Wisconsin to meet Nancy. She had much information to share. She had been actively researching the family tree for quite some time. Nancy took us on a tour of Fairchild and the surrounding area. Apparently, our great-great-grandfather helped to settle this small town in the late 1800s.

Nancy asked if I was interested in visiting a graveyard. She wanted to show me the gravestone of my great-grandmother. She wanted to know what it said on the gravestone, which was in German. It was an old cemetery, just off the side of the road a ways, not well kept.

We approached the grave of Wilhelmene. I was preparing to take a rubbing from the words written in German on the stone. As I touched the stone something strange occurred. I was immediately propelled in thought and emotion back to the sandbox. I saw the image of the younger woman in the simple tan dress. I immediately backed away from the stone. I was speechless. How could this be? Was it her? Was she one of the ladies who visited me that spring day in 1949? It said on the tombstone that she was born on 28 December 1860 and died 10 April 1894. She was only a little over thirty-three years old, but the mother of seven—one of them being my grandfather Gustav.

As I touched the stone again, the flashback memory of that day continued. It was her! I felt a sudden sense of love, of being hugged. How could this be? I continued to ask myself. Who was the other woman? Could it have been my great-great-grandmother Margaretha, the mother-in-law of Wilhelmene? I guess I will never know, but my thoughts that day convinced me that it was.

Later that fall my wife and I returned to Germany, but this time with the knowledge of my forefathers. We found my ancestral home of Breitscheid, near a small town called Bacharach where my great-great-grandparents were married in 1841. The church still stands. It was originally built in the 1300s. I entered the church and was taken by the emotion of the experience. The feeling of being home returned, only this time it was stronger. I still do not understand that feeling, and I am not a believer in reincarnation—but then, what do I know?

We met descendants of Grandpa's siblings who still live in that small village. It was wonderful. I finally had a connection and the knowledge that my genetic family was a loving and caring group of people. My original last name was nothing to be ashamed of.

The sandbox continues to be with me today. I was assured of my future and they were right. I believe those women who lovingly caressed my young cheek and spoke to me without words were sent by God. They were my grandmas and they came with a message.

Made in the USA
Lexington, KY
22 June 2010